Simon's voice grew more muffled. I guessed he was bending down and whispering to Plute just as I'd seen him do before.

I should have left then. Plute was back home – and my parents would be going mad wondering where I was.

How I wish I'd left then.

But I didn't. I wanted Simon to know it was me who'd brought Plute back.

The kitchen door was pushed open again. 'Now, stop it, you're still wet,' said Simon.

But Plute obviously didn't want to be dried. I could see the bottom half of his body wriggling about.

'Simon . . .' The word stopped in my mouth. As I'd seen something.

Then I saw it again, moving across Plute's back.

It was a hand. But a hand covered in hair. Thick, black, bristly hair. And the fingernails were very sharp and pointed – like claws . . .

Also available by Pete Johnson,
and published by Corgi Yearling Books:

THE GHOST DOG

MY FRIEND'S A
WEREWOLF

PETE JOHNSON

CORGI YEARLING BOOKS

MY FRIEND'S A WEREWOLF
A CORGI YEARLING BOOK : 0 440 863422

First publication in Great Britain

PRINTING HISTORY
Corgi Yearling edition published 1997

Set in 12½/15½pt Linotype New Century Schoolbook by Phoenix
Typesetting, Ilkley, West Yorkshire.

Corgi Yearling Books are published by Transworld Publishers Ltd,
61–63 Uxbridge Road, Ealing, London W5 5SA,
in Australia by Transworld Publishers (Australia) Pty. Ltd,
15–25 Helles Avenue, Moorebank, NSW 2170,
and in New Zealand by Transworld Publishers (NZ) Ltd,
3 William Pickering Drive, Albany, Auckland.

Made and printed in Great Britain by
Cox & Wyman Ltd, Reading, Berks.

This book is dedicated to:
Jan, Linda, Robin, Harry and Adam,
Bill Bloomfield and Sue Gregory

CHAPTER ONE

I thought werewolves only existed in stories and late-night films.

Now I know they are real.

It's an incredible story but I am going to tell you everything.

Then maybe you'll believe too.

I remember exactly when my story started. It was on a Saturday afternoon at the beginning of November. I was pretending to be tidying up my room when actually I was sitting on my bed reading a horror story. It was starting to get dark and

I was just drawing my curtains when the doorbell rang.

'Answer that, love, will you?' called my mum. 'Your dad's not back yet and I'm on the phone to your nan.'

I thumped down the stairs and opened the door to discover this boy I'd never seen in my life before, smiling shyly at me.

'Hello,' he said.

'Hello,' I replied cautiously.

He had curly black hair, very thick eyebrows and enormous dark green eyes. I guessed he was about thirteen, two years older than me.

'I've just moved in next door,' he said.

Mr and Mrs Atkins, who live next door in the end house, have gone to Germany for four years, so they've been letting their house out. The family who were there before never even said hello. They were horrible. We were all glad when they left.

'Do you go to the school down the road, Westcliffe High?' he asked.

I nodded.

'That's where I'm going. I'll be in Mrs Paine's class.'

'Same as me.' What made me think he was older than me? He wasn't especially tall. It must have been those little bits of stubble on his chin.

'So what's Mrs Paine like?' he asked.

'When she's in a bad mood she's a nightmare. And when she tells you off she spits right in your face. I want to say to her: tell me the news, not the weather.'

He started to laugh. 'I'm Simon, by the way.'

'And I'm Kelly.'

'Kelly,' he exclaimed. 'Why, that's a brilliant name.'

I was really surprised – and pleased – by his reaction, especially as a lot of people say I've got a dog's name and call out 'Here Kelly' and 'Walkies Kelly' when they're trying to be funny.

'Have you got any brothers or sisters?' he asked.

I shook my head.

'Neither have I.'

And I don't know why, but that seemed to create a little bond between us.

I invited him in. He was dressed casually in a blue sports shirt, baggy jeans, Kickers – and black gloves. My eyes kept going back to those black gloves. They had little pads under the fingertips and they just didn't fit in with what he was wearing. Those gloves looked weird somehow.

I took Simon into the kitchen. Muffin, our white cat, was sitting on the table. 'No, Muffin, bad cat,' I said. 'You know you're not supposed to be up there. Come on, down you get.'

To my surprise Muffin starting arching her back and hissing. She was hissing furiously at Simon as if he were her deadliest enemy.

'Muffin, stop that,' I began. But Muffin had already jumped off the table and fled away.

'I'm sorry about that,' I said. 'She's normally much friendlier.'

'She can probably smell my dogs off me. I've got four of them.'

'Four!' I exclaimed.

'Yeah, we had three dogs and now we've just got another one from the animal rescue centre. All my family are just mad about dogs.'

Soon we were chatting away as if we'd known each other for years. My mum and dad introduced themselves to Simon and afterwards pronounced him 'a very nice young lad'. Later Mum also popped next door to say hello, and to find out all the news. She came back saying how Mr and Mrs Doyle had moved here quickly because of Mr Doyle's new job. But if 'things worked out' they would settle in the area.

'Maybe Mr and Mrs Atkins might even sell them the house,' I said excitedly.

Next day Simon invited me round to his house for tea. There were still lots of unpacked boxes in the hallway. I dodged round them and followed Simon into the kitchen. I couldn't believe my eyes. There were platefuls of sausage rolls, sandwiches, cakes, biscuits.

'How many people are you expecting?' I cried.

'Only you,' said Simon.

'But there's enough food here for a party.'

'We just wanted you to feel welcome,' then with a grin he added, 'and we're not going to let you leave until you've eaten it all up.'

'I'll be here for weeks then.'

'That's fine . . . stay as long as you like,' he replied. Then Simon's parents appeared. His dad was very tall and balding while his mum was much smaller but with the same enormous green eyes as Simon. They both kept asking me if I was enjoying myself and seemed really disappointed when I said I couldn't eat any more.

I was about to leave when they insisted I have some hot chocolate, 'for the journey'. I didn't like to point out I was only going next door. Simon's dad brought in a tray of hot chocolate and still more biscuits which I couldn't even look at I was so full. Then Simon's mum asked, 'So, Kelly, is your bedroom at the front or the back of the house?'

I thought this was rather an odd question but I replied, 'At the back.'

At once, Simon's parents leaned forward and stared at me intently. 'Has Simon mentioned we've got four dogs?'

'Yes, I'd really like to see them.'

Simon's mum smiled. 'Well, we kept them away while you were eating, otherwise you wouldn't have got a moment's peace from them . . . At night they sleep outside in their kennel and they're good dogs but they can be a little noisy . . .'

'And we'd hate to think of them keeping you awake,' said Simon's dad.

'Oh, don't worry about that,' I replied at once. 'The neighbours before you were in a band, so I'd hear drums going at two in the morning. My dad said it was a real disgrace and he kept complaining but they never stopped. So after that, a few dogs barking is nothing.'

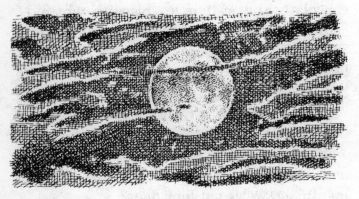

'Well, if ever they do disturb you, please tell us, won't you?' said Simon's dad.

'Yes, come straight to us,' said Simon's

mum, so firmly it was almost like a command.

I felt a little embarrassed by all this fuss. 'Look, I love dogs myself,' I began.

'Do you?' said Simon eagerly. 'Well, would you like to meet them?'

'Definitely.'

He charged off while his mum called after him: 'Make sure you check they haven't been digging in the mud . . .' She'd hardly finished speaking when three dogs tumbled through the doorway; the two West Highland terriers, yelping excitedly, dived straight on to Mrs Doyle's lap. 'Not both of you up here,' she said, but the dogs ignored her protests and made themselves comfortable. Meanwhile, the brown dog which Simon described as a 'sort of spaniel' circled excitedly around Simon, his tail thumping so hard he nearly sent a vase flying.

Then I spotted a fourth dog. A black labrador wagging his tail rather uncertainly in the doorway.

'That's Plute,' explained Simon. 'We've only had him a little while.'

'His last owners were unkind to him,' said

Simon's mum, 'so he's still a little bit unsure of himself.'

Simon went over to the dog, got down on his knees, put his face right up to Plute and started whispering to him. The dog seemed to be listening to him too. It was as if they were whispering secrets together.

Then Simon got to his feet and at once Plute came over to me. I stroked him gently and then he rolled over on to his back. 'See, he likes you,' cried Simon. 'I told Plute he would.' Later, Simon showed me the kennel in the garden where all the dogs slept.

'But it's huge,' I cried. 'Bigger than my bedroom.' Inside the kennel were all these thick rugs.

'We like our dogs to be comfortable,' said Simon.

'I bet it's funny when you take all four for a walk,' I said.

'It's mad,' laughed Simon, 'especially with Plute. You see, he's got this crazy hobby – he likes to chase cars.'

'Oh no.'

'Yeah, he's always trying to run off so he can go car chasing.' Simon rubbed Plute's head affectionately. 'He's such a nutty dog, that one.'

'Still, he's got a nice lot of space to run around in here,' I said. The whole garden was given over to grass. There were hardly any flowers at all but all round the garden were tall trees and bushes making it seem private and mysterious, almost like a secret garden. I liked that.

In fact, I felt really happy out there with Simon and all his dogs. Only one thing was bothering me. Simon was wearing those black gloves again. And they just looked so daft. I knew all my friends would think so too. Would he wear them to school tomorrow? He wouldn't be allowed, would he? I couldn't stop staring at them.

Finally, Simon said, 'You don't think

much of my gloves, do you?' He was looking straight at me when he said this.

'Oh no, they're . . .' I gulped hard. 'Well to be honest, I don't like them much,' I admitted finally.

'Nor do I,' said Simon. 'In fact I hate them. But I have to wear them. I've no choice. That's why I've got to take a letter into school tomorrow.' He sighed loudly. 'Shall we go back inside?'

I knew he didn't want to talk about it any more. But I couldn't help wondering what was wrong with his hands. Why did he have to keep them hidden in gloves all the time?

As I was leaving I said, 'I'll call for you for school tomorrow, if you like.'

'That'd be great,' he said eagerly.

'There's another person I call for, Jeff. He lives just up the road. I'm sure you'll like him.'

Simon nodded, then said, 'The dogs have really taken to you.'

'I like them very much too,' I replied.

Simon's face broke into a smile wide enough for two people. 'It's going to be so great us living next door to each other.'

I really agreed with him, then.

CHAPTER TWO

I was still waiting for my cereal to turn the milk all chocolatey – some days it just takes ages – when Simon bounded in.

'I'm early, aren't I?' His eyes were sparkling as if he was going to a party.

'Yes, and you're a bit keen,' I said.

'I know, sorry . . . but Kelly, I just can't wait.'

'To go to school? You're mad! So what was your old school like?'

The smile immediately faded off his face. 'It was OK, I guess. But I know this school is

23

going to be much better.' Then he grinned excitedly at me.

We set off to call for Jeff. I hoped Simon would like him and not judge by appearances. You see, Jeff is very small and very round and known to everyone as 'The Barrel'. When they're picking teams at school he's always the last to be chosen. In fact, no-one actually picks him they just say, 'And you've got The Barrel.'

Yet Simon was really friendly to Jeff, asking him questions about school and his hobbies – well, hobby. Jeff collects superhero comics. But Jeff gave these brief, almost rude answers and all the time spoke in this very flat tone.

We took Simon to the staffroom to see Mrs Paine. Outside the staffroom Jeff hissed, 'What about those black gloves he's wearing. I suppose he thinks he looks cool. Well, I think he looks pathetic.'

'That's so mean,' I replied. 'Simon has to wear those gloves.'

'Why?'

'I don't know exactly.'

'It's probably because his hands look

so horrible. I bet they're all greasy and wrinkled and got scabs all over them and . . .'

Jeff was interrupted by the staffroom door opening. Simon appeared. 'Well, she hasn't spat in my face yet,' he said.

I laughed, while Jeff just looked puzzled. Then I introduced Simon to some other people from my form. At first I think he was overwhelmed by this rush of new faces. But soon he was chatting away quite easily.

His arrival was certainly hot news. All day I was asked questions about him. It was good fun actually. Rat-bag Sarah even flounced up to me and said, 'Everyone's talking about you and Simon. Is he your boyfriend or not?'

Of course he wasn't my boyfriend but I wasn't going to tell Sarah that. So I just smiled mysteriously.

'And those gloves. Why? Are they glued to his hands?'

Again I smiled mysteriously. 'That's for me to know and you to find out.'

Sarah didn't like that answer at all. But in the afternoon she ran up to me again, smirking her head off.

'Simon's told me why he has to wear those gloves . . .' She lowered her voice dramatically. 'That fire he was in must have been terrible, mustn't it?'

For a moment I was too shocked to reply, then I said, 'Oh, yes, terrible,' and quickly walked away.

Fancy Simon telling Rat-bag Sarah about the fire he was in – and not me. I was really upset.

Later when I was walking home with Jeff and Simon I said, 'Sarah told me you got your hands burnt in a fire.'

'That's right,' he said shortly. Then he added, 'I really hate talking about it.' He shook his head. 'I had to tell her because she just kept on and on about it. They all did, all . . . except you.' He said those last words as if he were paying me a compliment.

'Sarah is just so nosy . . . I can't stand her actually,' I said.

'I think I like other people a lot more,' replied Simon, looking straight at me. I hoped I wasn't blushing.

Jeff gave this really loud whistle of annoyance; that was all Jeff said until we reached my house. Then he muttered, 'You haven't forgotten you're going to help me with maths homework, have you, Kelly?'

Actually Jeff is practically a genius at maths, so I knew this was his code for, I want to talk to you privately. We were hardly out of Simon's earshot when Jeff was hissing,

'Well, thanks a lot, Kelly. You've practically ignored me all day.'

'No, I haven't,' I replied indignantly.

'Yes you have; at lunchtime you went off with that Simon, leaving me all on my own.'

'I left you in a room full of people,' I cried. 'And I only went off to introduce Simon to some of the football team as he's interested in playing.'

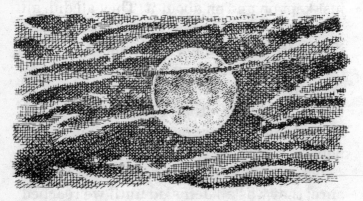

'Oh, is he?' said Jeff sarcastically. 'Well, isn't he just marvellous? I suppose old friends aren't good enough for you now?'

I felt a bit sorry for him – and just the tiniest bit guilty too. 'Oh, Jeff, don't be silly, it's only Simon is new so I have to look after him . . . and you do like him, don't you?'

'No.'

'No?' I was shocked.

'I think he's too good to be true.'

'Oh, what rubbish,' I began.

'There's something weird about him and you'd better be careful living next door to him.'

I gave a strange kind of laugh in reply. 'Well, everyone else likes him.'

Of course it helped that Simon was so brilliant at sports. I'd never seen anyone jump so high in basketball. He was also an amazingly fast runner and very soon was one of the stars of the football team. I stayed behind to cheer him on after school. So did quite a few other girls. Girls were always asking me questions about him and saying things like, 'I think you're so lucky having Simon move next door to you.'

I just smiled when they said that. But secretly I agreed with them. And then came the night of Sarah's fancy-dress party. Everyone from Sarah's form was invited – even me, although I think I was only invited because Sarah's mum and Jeff's mum are always round each other's houses and Sarah knew Jeff wouldn't go without me.

Simon said he had a great idea for his costume but wouldn't tell anyone what it was; he wanted it to be a surprise.

Jeff and I didn't have any ideas at all. Finally on Saturday afternoon we went into town hoping inspiration would strike.

Ever since Jeff and I had argued about Simon we hadn't been getting on too well. I was really upset about that – and I think Jeff was too. So this trip was also our way of making up.

But Jeff was acting really strangely. He'd bought this baseball cap which he was wearing round the wrong way and he kept telling me how tough and hard he was.

I just wished he'd be his usual self. We had hardly any money so we decided we'd just buy a mask at *Jolly Jokes Galore*. This shop was right on the edge of town and always looked dark and dreary. The paint was peeling off its sign. And inside there was an old, musty smell. A man in a grey overcoat glared fiercely at us. He had a very long red nose which Jeff was certain was false; he was always daring me to pull it.

We started looking through the masks of grinning clowns and famous people. All the ones I remembered from last time were still here, only covered in an extra layer of dust. Did he ever sell anything? I wondered.

Then Jeff exclaimed, 'Look at that!' and held up a mask I'd never seen before. It was of a werewolf.

It looked really horrible. The fur which hung down from the top and sides of the mask seemed real. So did the blood dripping from its long yellow fangs. I hated it. Yet I couldn't stop looking at it.

Then all at once Jeff put it on. His grey eyes glinted at me from the werewolf mask.

31

'This is what I'm wearing tonight,' he cried. 'I dare you to get one too.'

I hesitated.

'Go on,' he said. 'This is much better than going as some boring old clown.'

'All right,' I said slowly. I thought there might be only one werewolf mask in the shop, but the shopkeeper climbed up his step-ladder and solemnly brought down another one. He wrapped mine up. Jeff wore his out of the shop.

'At the party tonight,' he said, 'I'm going to jump out at people and say, '"I want your blood".'

'Vampires say that . . . not werewolves,' I corrected.

'I know,' said Jeff at once. 'What do werewolves say then?'

'They don't say anything, just growl a lot and attack people . . . and they howl, don't they?'

Immediately Jeff started practising his howl. He kept his mask on all the way home.

I didn't try my mask on again until I was getting ready to go out. I dressed all in black and I found these woolly gloves with long

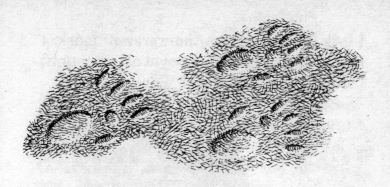

fingers – I suppose they looked a little like claws. Then I caught sight of myself in the mirror. I'm not one of those very pretty, sweet-looking girls like Rat-bag Sarah. My hair's my best feature – it's dark brown and quite long; it goes down past my shoulders now.

But otherwise I'm just normal, I suppose, except for my skin. It's deathly pale. Someone said once I looked like a ghost. I do try and brighten myself up, like recently I wore this really glittery dress to a party, Jeff immediately shouted out that I looked like an astronaut. I suppose an astronaut is better than a ghost.

Tonight, though, my skin seemed paler than ever. Sometimes I just hate the way

I look. Then I put on the werewolf mask. I looked a bit peculiar but not at all scary until I switched off the light.

At first the darkness seemed to swallow me up. I couldn't see anything at all. But then I started to make out the outline of a face. And suddenly I wasn't me any more. I was turning into someone else. I was turning into a monster. I gave a low howl. It sounded muffled, and surprisingly deep, nothing like my voice.

I shuddered.

Wouldn't it be awful if I couldn't change back – if I was doomed to wear this mask for the rest of my life. No-one would ever see me again. They'd always be running away from me. I gave another longer shudder.

Was the mask growing tighter?

It felt tighter.

I ran forward and switched on the light. At once I was just a girl in a mask from the joke shop again.

Then Jeff turned up. My dad was giving Jeff, Simon and me, of course, a lift to Rat-bag Sarah's party. At first Jeff and I were going to call round Simon's house in our masks. But then we thought it might be scarier if we hid in the back of the car and jumped out at him.

So Jeff and I hid underneath the back seat while Dad gave Simon a 'we're ready' toot on the car horn.

We crouched down in the darkness. I could feel Jeff's breath on my face. Then the car door opened. 'Hello, everyone,' said Simon.

'Well, hello Simon,' said Dad. 'I'm not sure where Jeff and Kelly have gone to,' he added. My dad always likes to join in our jokes.

Simon peered round enquiringly, and that was our cue to spring up, roaring and howling. And Simon just froze. He didn't laugh at us or pretend to be scared. He just stared and stared as if he couldn't believe his eyes.

'What do you think you're doing?' he said finally. His voice was shaking.

'We're being werewolves, of course,' replied Jeff indignantly.

Without another word Simon turned round to the front.

'What's wrong, Simon?' I asked.

He just shook his head. He didn't speak to us all the way to the party. Jeff kept whispering to me, 'You know what's wrong with him, don't you? He's jealous because our costumes are better than his.'

I found that hard to believe. Anyway, Simon's costume – tracksuit, boxing gloves and towel round his shoulders – was fine.

But something was certainly wrong.

We arrived to find the party in full swing. There was Batman, Superman and Superwoman, several pirates and pop stars and Sarah, as a ballerina! She pirouetted over to me. 'You and Simon have had a quarrel, haven't you?'

'No, why?'

'Oh, I just wondered,' she replied, before

pirouetting off again. She'd obviously noticed that Simon never came near Jeff and me all evening.

Jeff was having a great time, though, rushing round the party and jumping out at people. He seemed braver behind that mask. And when someone called him 'The Barrel', he gave this really loud, bloodthirsty howl, which made everyone at the party look round.

That was when Simon walked out of the party. I thought he'd just gone outside to get some fresh air or something. I went after him. But he'd gone. Later someone told me they'd seen him running up the road.

I told Jeff. He said, 'Oh, let him go, no reason to spoil our fun.'

But the party was ruined for me. Shortly afterwards I rang up my dad to pick us up.

When I arrived home I saw Simon. He was sitting on the wall in his front garden. He looked so sad I almost went over to him. But then I remembered I was angry with him for just running off like that without a word to me or Jeff. So I ignored him and quickly walked inside.

That night I woke up with a start. I always keep my window open at night. And although it has caused me major moth problems in the past (I used to hate it when moths would drop out of the air and on to my hair and once on to my mouth, but actually, they've got quite interesting faces up close), I love to fall asleep listening to that shimmering noise the wind makes rushing through the trees or the faraway whistle of a train. Or the new sound of dogs barking and yelping next door. Those noises relax me. It's only silence which keeps me awake.

But tonight there was a new noise.

One of the dogs was howling – and it was the saddest sound I'd ever heard. I wondered if it was Plute, the dog which had been badly treated before Simon's family adopted it. Was that dog remembering some cruelty now? The howling just went on and on.

I wanted to run next door and put my arms around poor Plute. But then I heard what sounded like Simon's parents outside and the howling stopped.

I hoped someone was patting Plute now.

Early next morning my dad said to me, 'Simon's at the door.'

I saw him waiting nervously for me in the doorway, hands clasped behind his back. 'Hello,' he said.

'Hello,' I said coldly.

'I'm sorry I ran off last night.'

'You didn't even say you were leaving. It was just so . . . rude.'

'I know.'

'So why did you do it?'

'I was upset,' he whispered.

'About what?' I demanded, but my tone was a little gentler now.

He stared at me as if he didn't know what to say then he stared down at the ground. He looked so awkward I couldn't help feeling a twinge of sympathy for him.

'Jeff reckoned you were jealous of our costumes,' I prompted.

'Yes, that was it,' he replied at once.

'But your costume was all right.'

'Not as good as yours though, and the fact you both had the same mask made me feel out of it, I suppose.'

I shook my head. 'That's so silly.' But I couldn't help smiling too.

'Anyway, these are for you,' he said, and from behind his back he produced a large box of chocolates with a large red ribbon on the box, and they still had the price on them as well, £4.50.

I'd never had a present from a boy before.

I felt all shivery. I hoped my face wasn't turning red. 'You shouldn't . . . but they're lovely,' I croaked. 'You'll have to help me eat them,' I added.

'I think that could be arranged,' he grinned. 'See you later.'

Then I called after him, 'Oh, by the way, was it Plute I heard howling last night?'

Simon looked startled.

'I heard a dog howling last night, so I thought . . .'

'Oh yes, that was Plute all right. Sorry he woke you up.'

'No, don't worry about that . . . it's just that he sounded so sad.'

'He's happier now,' replied Simon. 'Much happier.' And his green eyes shone so brightly they seem to cast their own light.

That afternoon Simon returned; between us we polished off the entire box of chocolates. I felt a bit sick afterwards – but very happy too.

Buying me those chocolates was such a sweet thing to do. Simon obviously had a heart of gold.

I decided to keep the empty packet, so I put it in the top drawer of my dressing-table with my other special presents and cards, but they were all from my mum and dad and other relations, like my nan. Somehow, this was even more special.

I never thought I'd throw it away. But I did, just two weeks later.

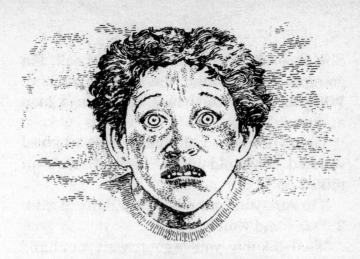

CHAPTER THREE

One week after Sarah's party I got the biggest shock of my life.

It was Friday afternoon and it was only Simon and me coming home from school that day, as Jeff was away with a bad cold.

We'd just turned into our road when Simon's mum came rushing up to us. 'You haven't seen Plute anywhere, have you?' she asked.

'No, why, what's happened?' demanded Simon.

'I just opened the door for a second,' said Mrs Doyle, 'and Plute shot straight past me.'

She shook her head and sighed. 'Look, I'm going to drive around. I'm sure I'll see him. Will you wait at the house, Simon, and keep an eye on the dogs?'

Then she rushed off again. Simon looked worried. 'Poor old Plute,' he said. 'He's all mixed up.'

'I'm sure your mum will find Plute,' I said. 'I'd stay and wait but . . .'

'Yeah, I know, you've got to visit your nan.' He smiled. 'Have a good time.'

'I won't. I'll see you tomorrow – and Plute.'

'That's right,' he said, but he still looked anxious.

At home Mum and Dad were waiting for me. 'At last,' cried Dad. 'Well, get changed as quick as you can. We told your nan we'd be there for five o'clock and you know how she worries if we're late.'

My nan is totally ancient. This is quite handy when you're doing history projects on the War of the Roses or something, as she loves reminiscing – especially about her time in Cornwall. She'd lived there for years.

But after Grandad died, Nan moved near

us. She now lives in this little cottage with a huge garden, and whenever you visit her you have to walk around it – admire all her plants and vegetables.

Still, I quite enjoy visiting Nan – even though she hasn't got a television, just a crackly old radio which has always got discussions on it about how to get moss off your grass.

But today I wanted to stay at home and wait for Plute, only I knew my parents would never let me do that. So I reluctantly put on my 'going to see ancient relatives' clothes. Mum asked me to fetch her scarf. I went into my parents' bedroom and glanced idly out of the window, noticing it was starting to rain. Then I saw something which made me forget all about my mum's scarf: Plute.

He was running right in the middle of the road, chasing after every car which passed him. But he could get killed doing that. I sped downstairs.

'Where are you going, Kelly?' demanded my dad.

'Got to get Plute.' And before he could reply I ran like crazy up the road.

'Plute, here Plute, come on boy,' I called. A car swerved to avoid Plute; the owner yelled out of the window at me, 'That dog should be on a lead.'

'I know,' I yelled back. 'Sorry.'

Then for a moment, the road was clear. I raced over to Plute. 'Good boy, come on then, Plute,' I murmured, while half-dragging him on to the pathway. He wagged his tail cautiously at me. Then a car passed and Plute let out a low growl. I gave him a hug. 'What were you doing running in the road like that?' I whispered. 'Still, you were coming home, weren't you?'

As if in agreement, Plute wagged his tail more enthusiastically. 'Come on then, Plute, let's take you back and out of this rain.' For it was raining quite hard now. And with one

46

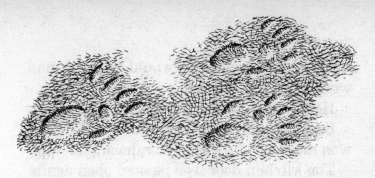

hand still on his collar I led him down the road. Plute clearly recognized his house because as soon as we drew near he yelped excitedly.

'Yes, that's your home all right,' I said, 'and Simon's going to be so pleased to see you back.'

To my surprise the front door was ajar so I let Plute rush ahead of me. He obviously knew exactly where Simon was. The kitchen door was one of those swing doors, so Plute could nudge it open. Chart music burst out of the kitchen followed by Simon's voice exclaiming, 'Plute, where have you been? Look at you, you're all wet.' The door swung half-shut and Simon's voice grew more muffled. I guessed he was bending down and whispering to Plute just as I'd seen him do before.

I should have left then. Plute was back

47

home – and my parents would be going mad wondering where I was.

How I wish I'd left then.

But I didn't. I wanted Simon to know it was me who'd brought Plute back.

The kitchen door was pushed open again. 'Now, stop it, you're still wet,' said Simon.

But Plute obviously didn't want to be dried. I could see the bottom half of his body wriggling about.

'Simon . . .' The word stopped in my mouth. As I'd seen something.

Then I saw it again, moving across Plute's back.

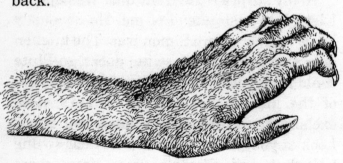

It was a hand. But a hand covered in hair. Thick, black, bristly hair. And the finger-nails were very sharp and pointed – like claws.

I'd only ever seen a hand like this once before. It was in the window of *Jolly Jokes Galore*. It was called *The Monster's Claw*. I remember Jeff saying to me, 'If that claw was real, it could rip your ear off with one swipe.'

And I'd shivered when Jeff had said that even though I'd known it wasn't real. There was something about it which made me uneasy.

But this claw . . . what was it?

WHAT WAS IT?

'Where did you find Plute, Mum?' Simon's voice. I couldn't reply. I couldn't move.

Simon pushed the kitchen door open a little further. 'Mum,' he began. Then he gazed up at me. And at once all the colour fell from his face.

Plute bolted away with the towel sliding off his back while Simon slowly got to his feet. I let out a thin cry when I saw him, saw both his terrible claws.

The monster's claws.

I started to back away from him.

'Kelly, wait!' he shouted. For a second I glimpsed an ashen face staring into mine.

But then my eyes returned to those hideous claws.

'I've got to go,' I croaked, looking behind me for the door which was suddenly a thousand miles away.

'All right, run away then,' he cried suddenly. 'I don't blame you. Who wouldn't run from these?' He raised both his hands in front of him. 'Who wouldn't be scared?'

'I'm not scared,' I gasped. 'I've just got to go home. Truly I have.'

'Oh, Kelly,' he said, 'you really weren't meant to see this.' He shook his head sadly, then walked back inside the kitchen, closing the door behind him.

This was my chance to escape from the monster. I should have sprinted out of there right away. But Simon wasn't a monster. He was my friend: someone whom I liked very much. He would never harm me, would he?

I was all confused.

'I thought you'd gone,' said Simon, standing in the kitchen doorway. He was watching me with a curious expression on his face.

'No . . . no,' I spluttered. Then I started edging towards the front door again.

He raised his hands; they were hidden in his black gloves again now. 'No-one's ever supposed to see what lies behind these gloves.'

'Well, don't worry about me. I hardly saw a thing really.'

'I'm only supposed to take these gloves off at night, but my hands get so hot and sticky and they itch, too . . . So how did you get in here?' he demanded suddenly.

'The door was open so . . .'

He gave a groan. 'I must have been so worried about Plute I forgot to shut it . . . You brought Plute back, didn't you?'

'Yes, he was running in the road. I saw him.' My voice kept trembling.

51

'I wish you'd stop looking at me like that.'

'Like what?'

'Like I'm about to eat you up.'

I laughed shakily. 'Don't be silly.'

'Well, come a bit nearer then.'

I moved forward about one millimetre. Plute appeared again; he stood beside Simon panting excitedly. Simon bent down and patted him, then whispered, 'It's because of you Kelly knows my terrible secret. You've given me away, Plute.' Then he looked up at me. 'The doctors told me in a couple of years my hands will be back to normal. So I've just got two more years of this.' He gave this really unhappy laugh. 'I'm counting the days off on my calendar, I really am. I hate being a freak.'

'You're not a freak, Simon,' I said softly.

His large, green eyes stared intently at me. Then he whispered to Plute, 'I told you she was my friend, didn't I?' Still gazing down at Plute, he whispered, 'Can I ask you a big favour?'

'What's that?' I replied, my voice nearly as low as Simon's.

'Don't tell anyone what you saw today. Will you promise me that one thing? Please.'

Before I could reply the doorbell sounded, making me jump. And then I heard my mum call, 'Sorry to barge in but . . . Kelly, what are you thinking of? You're supposed to be round your nan's. You can see Simon tomorrow. Oh, Simon, I know your mum and I only exchanged keys for emergencies, but the plumber still hasn't called. If he turns up would you ask your mum to let him in, only . . .' My mum rattled on while I stood there in a daze.

I spent the next few hours like that.

'You're very quiet,' said my nan to me that evening. 'And you've hardly eaten anything.' She felt my forehead, then announced to my mum, 'Yes, the child is definitely sickening for something.'

53

'Well, her friend Jeff is away from school and I thought Simon looked a bit peaky this afternoon; there's obviously something going round. How do you feel, dear?'

'I do feel a bit groggy,' I said. This wasn't a lie – although I knew I wasn't ill.

On the way home my parents put a thick blanket around me. I sat in the back of the car thinking, thinking, thinking. If only I'd seen scabs or scars or hundreds of spots on Simon's hands – they were the sort of nasty things anyone could get.

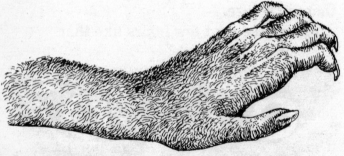

But I'd never seen hands as hairy as Simon's. It was almost as if he'd had an animal's hands grafted on to his body.

I shivered.

But he said it was all caused by some medical ailment. Why couldn't I believe him?

I did believe him. I just wanted more proof. Maybe my parents would know. 'Mum, is there a medical condition which makes your hands go all hairy?'

'Hey, watch out, I've got hairy hands,' said Dad.

'No, I don't mean like that. I mean masses and masses of hair.'

Mum turned and smiled. 'I think you've been reading too many spooky stories.'

Dad added, 'If you ever see anyone with hands like that, Kelly, run for your life.' Then he and Mum roared with laughter.

I stared miserably outside at the dark, rainy night and the cars swishing past. The windscreen wipers whirled backwards and forwards and they seemed to be saying: run for your life. Over and over they repeated it: *Run for your life. Run for your life. Run for your life.*

Next day was Saturday. My parents fussed over me, saying how pale and drawn I looked. In the afternoon, just to get away from them, I said I wanted to go for a walk.

They finally decided a bit of fresh air might do me good. 'Why don't you call for Simon?' said my mum.

'Yes, yes,' I murmured. I didn't know whether to or not. It was already getting dark outside. I hate it when the days get swallowed up so quickly.

I walked past Simon's house. He was sitting at a table in front of the window, writing. A pale yellow lamp was on beside him. It made the whole room look warm and welcoming. Then he looked up and saw me. He immediately signalled that I should come in.

Why shouldn't I go in? Simon was my friend.

I followed him through to the room where he had been writing.

'You're not doing homework, are you?' I said.

'No, I'm writing to Lawrence, a good mate of mine.'

I nodded, interested. Simon hardly ever spoke about his friends. 'Did he used to go to your old school?'

'Yes, that's right,' said Simon vaguely.

'So where was your old school?'

'Cornwall,' he muttered.

'Oh, really, my nan used to live there, back in the Dark Ages.'

Simon grinned and changed the subject. Then his mum came in, made the fire up for us and insisted I had some hot chocolate as I 'looked perished'.

We sat on the couch in front of the fire. We chatted about school and how much Simon liked playing for the school football team. I tried to relax but I felt nervous and awkward somehow. I think Simon did as well. For he suddenly whispered, 'You didn't tell anyone about . . . yesterday?'

'No,' I replied firmly.

'I knew you'd keep your promise,' he said warmly. 'If anyone had to find out I'm glad it was you.'

I blushed at the compliment. 'Did you tell your parents?' I asked.

A look of horror crossed his face. 'Oh no, they'd go mad – especially my mum. She'd hit the roof.'

I shivered without quite knowing why. His mum reappeared with a tray of hot chocolate and biscuits.

'Make sure you drink it all now, won't you, Kelly?' she said.

Why was she so keen on me having this hot chocolate? Because Simon did tell her what I'd seen and now she wants to poison me? At once I knew I was being totally silly.

But even so, I sipped the hot chocolate very slowly. The dogs raced around us begging for food, and we talked about other things. But I couldn't get what I'd seen out of my mind.

'About yesterday,' I said. 'There was just one thing I wanted to ask you.'

'Keep your voice down,' whispered Simon.

Then with a trace of irritation, 'What is it, then?'

'I just wanted to know the proper name of your illness.' For then I thought to myself I could look it up.

'What an odd question,' said Simon, looking suddenly quite fierce. 'What does it matter anyway.'

'Oh, it doesn't,' I said quickly.

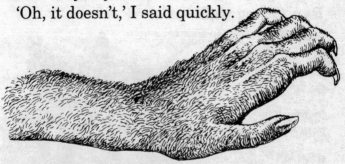

'OK, my hands are different to yours. I've got this – well I wouldn't even call it an illness – but anyway, it's not infectious. You'll never get it, so what does it matter what it's called. I'm the same person I was before you found out.' His voice rose. 'I'm still me.'

The door opened. His mum looked in. 'Everything all right?'

'Fine, thanks, Mum.'

'Good, good,' she murmured, looking all around the room. Nice as his mum was, I felt as if she was checking up on us – or me.

I wondered again if Simon had told her about yesterday. There was something going on in this house, wasn't there? Something I didn't know about. Then Dad's words started echoing around in my head: *Run for your life. Run for your life.*

I sprang to my feet. 'I've got to go,' I announced.

'What, already?' exclaimed Simon.

'Yeah, I told my parents I'd only be ten minutes, so I'm already in trouble . . . I'll let you get back to your letter.'

'OK then, well, come round anytime.'

'Thanks.' I fled before his mum could appear again.

That night I really wanted to tell my parents everything, but I couldn't. That would be like sneaking on Simon. Besides, I'd promised.

Then I suddenly remembered I'd never actually promised Simon anything. The doorbell had gone before I could say anything. Still, Simon thought I'd promised him. And that was the same thing.

Or was it?

CHAPTER FOUR

On Monday morning I walked to school with Simon. We chatted about the new number one in the charts (we both hated it), a thriller which had started on television last night, and oh, so many things. It was a perfectly ordinary conversation. So why did I feel we were both acting?

Jeff was still away from school. I missed him. I'd meant to go and visit him last night. But then I figured Jeff would realize something was worrying me right away – he's pretty quick like that – and before I knew it

63

I'd be blurting out Simon's secret. And I really didn't want to do that.

If only – if only Simon would tell me the name of the illness which had turned his hands into . . . claws.

That's all I needed to know. And if Simon really was my friend he'd tell me, trust me.

I decided to have one last go. 'Simon, can I ask you something?'

He turned sharply as if sensing what I was going to ask. And he looked so hurt as if I was about to let him down.

I swallowed hard. 'So when are you playing for the school football team again?'

Immediately the atmosphere relaxed. And then we met two of the boys from the football team. They really liked Simon. Everyone did – except Jeff. But would they be patting Simon on the back now and laughing and joking with him if they knew his secret? Would they even be talking to him?

Simon gave me one of his big smiles. 'See you later, Kelly,' he said. He was acting as if everything was just the same.

But it wasn't.

To be honest, I was glad when Simon went

off with his mates. I needed time to think. I walked into school, and down the long corridor to my form-room.

'Hello, Kelly,' called a voice.

'Hello,' I replied absently, lost in thought. Then I realized who it was. It was the school nurse. I looked up, amazed at how she seemed to remember everyone's name.

And then I had an idea.

The school nurse could tell me if Simon was lying or not. I wouldn't mention him by name, of course. I'd just ask her casually if there was an illness which turned your hands all hairy. That wouldn't do any harm, would it?

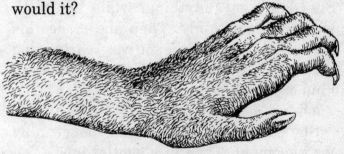

I went over to her: 'Excuse me . . . can I ask you something, please?' My voice was shaking all over the place.

'Yes, of course, Kelly, come in.'

She was a large woman with a very red face and false teeth which moved up and down every time she spoke. I went inside her room. There was nowhere to sit except for this couch in the corner. And I didn't want to lie down as if I were ill or something. But then she found me a chair.

I felt nervous. 'What it is,' I began, then all in a rush, 'This sounds a bit of a silly question, but is there an illness which makes your hands turn hairy, I mean, really hairy – and your nails go all pointed and sharp too?' I paused for breath.

The nurse just opened her mouth wide. She didn't say anything, while her teeth wobbled uncertainly. Then she made this sucking noise – I think she was rearranging her teeth – and asked sharply, 'Is this some kind of joke?'

'Oh no,' I cried.

She sucked her teeth again thoughtfully for a moment. Then in a gentler tone, 'You know, Kelly, there was a boy at my school who claimed his hands had turned purple. He got us girls proper scared. It turned out it was just the dye from his gloves but it looked most realistic. I must say he had me fooled. I'm assuming it's a boy this time too.'

I nodded.

'Boys don't change, do they? He's pulling your leg, love. You tell him, if he's got hands like that Nurse wants to see them, he's a medical marvel.' She got up. 'You cut along to your lesson now. I think we've wasted enough time on your friend, don't you?'

Part of me wanted to tell Nurse that I'd seen those hands with my own eyes, but I couldn't do that. Still, at least I knew for certain Simon had been lying to me.

An angry tear crept down my face. I quickly brushed it away. And then I saw Simon. He was leaning against the wall opposite the school nurse's room. What was he doing there? Was he following me?

'Someone said they'd seen you go in the

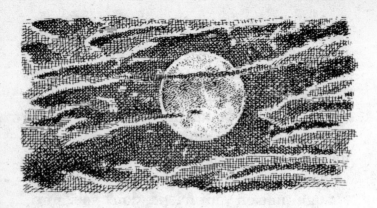

nurse's room. Are you all right?'

'I'm all right,' I muttered. I wasn't going to tell him anything so I just walked away from him, brushing away another angry tear. Then I turned round. He was still staring after me. A cold shudder crept up my back. I practically ran to my form-room.

That night I went round to Jeff's house. Jeff's mum was standing outside talking to their next-door-neighbour, Mr Prentice, an oldish man with a very large, egg-shaped head and no neck, so he looked as if he were permanently shrugging his shoulders. He spent most of his time now staring out of the window. He even ate his meals looking out of that window. He used to be a big-game hunter, or so he claimed. Certainly his house was full of stuffed animals which I thought was creepy and horrible.

'Ah, come to visit the young invalid, have we?' he said.

I hate it when people talk to me in that patronizing way. So I just answered, 'That's right,' and stared at Jeff's mum.

'Go straight up, dear,' she said. 'I'm sure Jeff will be very pleased to see you.'

But when I opened Jeff's bedroom door he called out very sarcastically, 'Oh, how nice of you to come round. I thought you'd forgotten who I was.'

'Don't be silly,' I replied. 'You know I had to go to my nan's on Friday.'

'And Saturday, and Sunday.'

'I was busy then too.'

'Well, I'm glad someone was enjoying themselves.' His voice was hoarse and his nose was bright red.

'Are you still feeling bad?'

'Terrible.' He blew his nose vigorously as if to prove it. 'Why do I get more colds than anyone I know? My sisters never get colds' – Jeff had two sisters, both older than him –

69

'and they're always out somewhere. It's not fair.'

'I brought you these. I wasn't sure if you already had them.' I handed Jeff two super-hero comics.

He glanced at them. 'I have got them, actually. I must have every superheroes comic in the world, but thanks, anyway. Sit down – and get rid of her, will you?' He nodded at a woman who was babbling away on his little black-and-white television set.

I switched her off and sat down on the edge of Jeff's bed.

'So, got any hot news for me?' he demanded. 'I've been bored out of my skull up here.'

'Well, actually I have . . . it's about Simon.'

Immediately Jeff sank down in his bed again. 'Don't tell me, he played for the school team on Saturday morning and scored eighty-seven goals with his eyes shut.'

'No, nothing like that,' I said.

Jeff looked at me. A light came into his eyes. 'What's up, Kelly?' he asked.

'It's a secret, actually. It's . . .' I stopped. I felt as if I was about to betray Simon. But

70

Simon had lied to me, so my promise to him didn't hold any more. It wasn't even a real promise anyway. 'If I tell you this secret, do you promise not to tell anyone else?'

'Yes, all right, just get on with it.'

Then I told Jeff everything. And it was such a relief. At last someone else knew. When I'd finished Jeff shook his head. 'This is a wind-up, isn't it?'

'No, it's not a wind-up,' I replied firmly.

Jeff let out a low whistle of amazement and said, 'Well then, he's a werewolf.'

At that we both burst out laughing. Finally, I said lightly, 'How could he be a werewolf?'

'He's hairy enough to be one,' said Jeff. 'Imagine shaking hands with him.'

'Oh, don't be horrible.'

Jeff grinned. 'Do you suppose, in the morning his mum goes, "Now Simon, have you brushed your hair and your hands?"'

I giggled. 'And when he goes to the hair-dresser's, do you think he gets his hands cut too?'

'Probably has them shampooed,' said Jeff. We started laughing again at the absurdity of it all.

'I've just thought of something,' said Jeff. 'Do you remember when we wore those were-wolf masks and he got the hump about it – well, maybe he thought we were on to him.'

'No . . .' I began.

'Well, it could be. After all, your bedroom does look out on to their back garden. And no-one else could see past all their trees and stuff. Only you.'

I gulped, then said slowly, 'You won't tell anyone, will you, Jeff? You promised.'

'All right,' he muttered. 'But I reckon I should keep a log of all this, just in case . . .'

'In case of what?'

'Well, with those claws he could rip your head off without blinking,' said Jeff.

'Oh, thanks,' I cried.

Jeff leaned forward eagerly. 'And if a werewolf sinks its teeth into you, you become one too. And I saw this film recently where they scratched someone and that's pretty bad too. You . . .'

'All right, all right,' I interrupted. 'Look, aren't we forgetting something here? We're talking about Simon. Our friend.'

'Well, he's more your friend than mine.'

'Who's got this medical condition . . .'

'Which no-one has ever heard of.' Then, seeing my face, 'OK, Simon might just be seriously weird. But there's no harm in being careful, is there? That's why I'm going to write down everything that's happened and then put on the front: "This is strictly private. Only to be read in emergencies, like getting your head ripped off." That's a joke,' he added quickly. 'By the way, are you going to tell Simon I know?'

'Er . . . well . . .'

'Only it's probably best I'm undercover.' Jeff picked up a notebook. 'Now, I want to get every detail written down.'

Later that evening, when I was back home, Jeff rang me. 'I'm speaking on my dad's mobile,' he said proudly. 'Have you got anything to report?'

'Not yet.'

'I've written it all up now, seven and a half pages . . . I also wanted to tell you to keep your bedroom window closed tonight.'

'Why?'

'It's best not to take any risks with a werewolf about.'

'So what do you think it's going to do, leap into my room in the middle of the night?'

Straightaway I wished I hadn't said that, especially when Jeff replied, 'Werewolves can jump very high, you know, and . . .'

'Jeff, goodnight,' I replied, slamming the

phone down. What had started as a joke – making out Simon was a werewolf – wasn't funny any more. I had a feeling Jeff had started to believe it.

Just because someone's got hairy hands and long fingernails doesn't mean they're a werewolf, does it? I felt ashamed of myself for telling Jeff now.

That night I fell asleep almost at once, but then I woke up with a start. I knew there was something in my bedroom. I'd heard it move.

I froze with horror.

Once before I'd heard something at night. And then I'd seen it waddling along the carpet. The shock made me scream. My dad came racing to my room and then we both tried to catch it – a bird that had flown in through my window.

'Don't hurt it,' I cried as my dad lunged for it. But it kept fluttering away. My dad said it was like trying to get hold of a bar of soap. We were ages. Finally I caught the bird. I remember, it had tiny pink legs. Then with a flurry of feathers the bird soared out of my hands and into the cold night. Had another bird flown in tonight?

My eyes were getting used to the dark now. I sat up and peered cautiously around my room. Then I stared down at the carpet. Something stared back at me.

The most hideous face I'd ever seen.
This time I was too scared even to scream.
I knew I mustn't move. I must keep as still

as possible. But I couldn't stop my heart thumping. It was deafening. I'd seen something so horrible and nasty . . . and all at once I knew what it was. I stared down at that face again – its jaws open wide, showing all its cruel teeth.

It was my werewolf mask.

It must have fallen off the back of the door. And the noise of its falling must have woken me. Funny how it's often the tiniest little sounds which wake you up, isn't it?

I knew, though, that I couldn't sleep with that hideous face lying on my carpet. I had to tuck it away in the cupboard. But first, I wanted the light on. I climbed out of bed. I knew the mask wasn't real but I still crept gingerly round it, just in case it suddenly moved.

My bedroom's quite small but tonight my journey to the light switch seemed to take a million years. My hand reached for the switch then something brushed against my legs. I gazed down in terror to see Muffin staring up at me.

'Oh, Muffin, don't do that,' I gasped. I switched on the light. But the room still wasn't bright enough. I sat on the edge of my bed with Muffin beside me. I stroked her head. 'You shouldn't have sneaked in like that, but I'm really pleased to see you. You can be my bodyguard tonight.'

I bent down and picked up the tip of the werewolf mask and then flung it into the back of my cupboard. Tomorrow, I thought to myself, I would chuck it out.

I was just climbing back into bed when this howling noise started. Muffin immediately stiffened and started hissing.

'Don't be afraid,' I whispered. 'It's only Plute – a sad, lonely dog.'

Yet Plute sounded different tonight: louder and fiercer, like a wild beast declaring its supremacy. I shivered. Then I became angry with myself. Plute wasn't a wolf. He was a tame labrador with a weakness for chasing cars. Wolves don't exist – not in Britain anyway.

And werewolves don't exist anywhere. I looked around for Muffin. She'd gone. 'Muffin,' I whispered. Then I spotted my 'bodyguard' crouching underneath my bed. I tried coaxing her out. But Muffin wouldn't budge.

Meanwhile that howling noise grew louder. Now it seemed to fill my room. What was it?

It was a werewolf.

What nonsense.

But I suddenly sprang up and closed my window tightly. Now the noise was much fainter. I took a deep breath. Then I saw Muffin emerge from her hiding place. I picked her up and put her on to the bed.

I sat stroking her for a while. Usually after a few minutes Muffin will jump down and go on her way. But tonight she stretched herself right out on to my legs. I think she was still scared.

She wasn't the only one.

CHAPTER FIVE

Next morning Muffin had gone. And my room felt very stuffy. So I got up and opened the window a little. I heard the whirr of the milk-float and the crates rattling. Those noises reassured me.

I decided I'd over-reacted last night. Just because I'd heard a dog howling I'd started imagining things. It was pretty silly really. Still, the first thing I did after I got up was hurl that werewolf mask in the bin.

Dad was on holiday this week, so over breakfast he was boasting about all the decorating he was going to do. 'You won't recognize the bathroom when I've finished,' he said.

'We'll believe that when we see it, won't we, Kelly?' said Mum, winking at me.

'I wouldn't be surprised if Dad is still sitting here when I get back from school,' I replied.

It was fun teasing Dad. It made last night seem far away. Then the telephone rang. It was Jeff.

'Any news?' he asked breathlessly.

'Well . . . I heard this howling noise . . .'

'That's him, Simon the werewolf,' cried Jeff. 'I hardly got a wink of sleep last night you know, thinking about it all – and finding out things. Did you know that tonight is a full moon?'

That news took me by surprise. 'No, I didn't.'

'I also wanted to warn you,' whispered Jeff urgently.

'Warn me?'

'Well, if Simon is a werewolf – he'll want to make sure you keep his secret, won't he?'

'I suppose so,' I said cautiously.

'So he might do something to prove his

power and say, "Don't mess with me."'

'Like what?' I said in a small gasp.

'I think he'll kill – well, he might kill Muffin, for a start.'

'What?' I cried, and immediately started looking for Muffin.

His voice rose. 'I'm not saying it will be Muffin definitely. I just think he will do something.'

The doorbell rang.

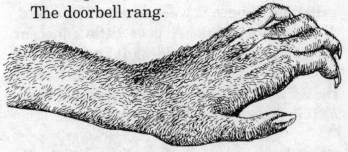

'Answer that, will you, Kelly?' called Mum.

'Is that him?' asked Jeff.

'I expect so,' I replied. 'Anyway, thanks very much for ringing. You've really cheered me up.'

'I'm only trying to help.' Jeff was indignant. 'I've been up all night thinking about this.'

'Well, anyway, look on the bright side. If Simon really is a werewolf, at least we know what to get him for his birthday: a razor.' I sniggered at my little joke. But Jeff didn't.

'Just be careful, Kelly, won't you?'

He sounded so scared I felt scared too – for about a second. But then I laughed to myself. Jeff was talking rubbish – as usual. I opened the door. And then I saw . . .

I knew at once it was dead. It was a bird. A thrush, I think. A poor little innocent thrush. Simon was holding it in his gloved hand. But he was waving the dead bird in the air as if he was proud of what he'd done, as if it were some kind of trophy.

Simon was also saying something to me. But I couldn't listen to him. I was too upset, too horrified by his crime. 'How could you have killed that bird?' I screamed at him. 'How could you?' I screamed so loudly my mum and dad rushed out of the kitchen.

'Whatever's happened?' began my mum. Then she saw Simon standing there with the bird in his hand and immediately declared, 'Oh no, not again. That's the third time this month Muffin has done that. I'm always telling her off about it.'

'I'm afraid it's a cat's nature,' said my dad, sadly. 'Did you find it on the step, Simon?'

He nodded gravely. 'It looked so awful just lying on the step. I thought it would be best to bury it.' Simon spoke quite calmly but his hand was shaking.

'I think Muffin leaves them there as a kind of present,' said Mum. 'It's a thrush, and they're so tame as well.' Then she turned to me. 'In the past you've always been at school. I know it is upsetting to see.' Mum gave my hand a squeeze. 'Why don't we bury the thrush by the bushes over there?'

I stood in the doorway and watched while

Mum, Dad and Simon dug a little hole for the bird. It had been horrible seeing that poor, dead bird. But something else upset me too. It was my thinking Simon had killed it. I felt so ashamed.

Dad insisted on driving us to school as he thought I 'still looked a bit shaky'. Simon and I sat in the back. We didn't say one word to each other. Dad obviously thought I was still in shock and rattled on about 'nature's chain'.

'Keep an eye on her, Simon,' said Dad when we reached the school gates.

As soon as Dad had gone Simon said, in a horrible, choked kind of voice, 'You really thought I'd killed that bird, didn't you?'

I was so full of shame and embarrassment I could hardly look at him. 'No, Simon . . . no, I didn't. It's just, well, I didn't sleep very well last night and the way you were holding it made me . . .'

'Oh, come on, at least be honest,' cut in Simon, harshly.

In a flash I retorted, 'Like you've been honest with me, like you've told me the truth about your hands. No-one's heard about that illness you mentioned.'

'What do you mean?' gasped Simon. 'You haven't told anyone my secret?'

'No, well not exactly. I mean, I didn't mention you by name.' That, of course, was a lie. I became confused and embarrassed again. I looked up at him almost pleadingly. 'It's just that what you told me . . . it doesn't make any sense,' I began. But then I saw his huge, green eyes. They were alight with fury. I couldn't help noticing something else; his face seemed much hairier this morning. He had the beginnings of a small moustache now and there was hair growing on his neck too.

I stepped back.

'You'd better not have told anyone,' he said, his voice low and menacing.

'Why, what are you going to do?' I taunted,

but I sounded much braver that I felt. Before he could reply a group of boys came up. 'Three–one,' they chanted. 'Spurs was annihilated on Saturday.'

'No, we played well. We just didn't get the chances,' replied Simon. He went off, laughing and arguing with them. Only this time he didn't say 'See you later' or smile at me.

He didn't even turn round . . .

Why should he? We weren't friends any more.

I certainly didn't want to walk home with him after school. But as it happened, during break, Simon ran out of the form-room saying he had a really bad headache.

Later I heard his mum had taken him home.

When I arrived home Mum said, 'There's someone waiting to see you,' and I jerked in horror, thinking it was Simon. But, instead, it was Jeff.

'I'm feeling a bit better so your mum's invited me round for tea . . . not that I've quite got my appetite back,' he added, piteously. 'But I think I could manage something.' In fact, Jeff managed two platefuls of fish fingers, chips and baked beans and a large helping of fruit trifle. Afterwards we escaped to my room where I gave Jeff a full report of what had happened during the day.

When I'd finished Jeff looked at me for a moment, then said significantly, 'I don't think Simon went home because he had a headache . . . it was because he was turning into a complete and total werewolf. I mean, you said he looked a bit hairier first thing this morning, didn't you?'

'Yes, that's true.'
'Well, he could probably sense more hair was about to sprout up so he had to get out of school fast. By now I bet his face and body will be totally covered in hair.'

I started to picture this while Jeff went on, 'He'll have hair everywhere now. In fact, he probably won't be able to see very well, he'll have so much fur hanging over his eyes. You wouldn't recognize him tonight, Kelly.' Then his voice became graver. 'But you're in danger, especially now he knows you haven't kept his secret. Simon probably suspects you've told me. So I'm in danger as well. When I go home tonight he could be waiting to jump out at me or something.' He gave a nervous laugh. 'We'll have to tell someone, like your parents – or mine.'

I got up. My head was in a whirl. 'I don't know,' I began.

'We've got to.'

'But what can I tell them?'

Jeff gave an impatient gesture. 'How

about that your next-door-neighbour has got claws for hands and is at the moment turning into a full-scale werewolf?'

'No,' I said, firmly, 'that would be really sly.'

'Sly,' echoed Jeff contemptuously.

'Yes, I mean we don't know for certain Simon is a werewolf.'

'How much more evidence do you need?' cried Jeff.

'You want him to be a werewolf, don't you?'

'And you still really like him, don't you?' replied Jeff.

We stood staring accusingly at each other until I suddenly laughed. 'Do you remember when you thought there was a monster at the bottom of the garden?'

'Oh, that was millions of light years ago.'

'You even went and told your mum there was a monster there. And she just said, "Oh, that's nice, dear."'

'Well I think that's charming bringing that up,' said Jeff. But he couldn't help laughing too.

'So maybe, Jeff, when you tell your mum

about that werewolf she'll just go, "Oh, that's nice, dear."'

Jeff seemed to smile and frown at the same time. 'The trouble is, adults never check things out. I mean, they won't go and pull Simon's gloves off and see for themselves. What we need is more evidence.'

Out of his sports bag (although Jeff hates sports), he produced the log-book – 'We must write everything down in here' – and a pair of binoculars. 'They're not brilliant but they might help us keep watch. You don't mind if I stay over, do you, Kelly?'

'Of course not. I'd be really happy if you did actually.'

Jeff grinned at me. 'Werewolves have to be outside during a full moon so I'm sure we'll see something tonight.' Then he got up. He was so excited he couldn't stand still. He was practically dancing around my room.

But then our plan hit a snag. Jeff's mum wouldn't let him stay over. In fact she wouldn't let him stay past seven o'clock. She said he still hadn't built his strength up and needed a good night's rest.

So despite all his pleading, Jeff had to go. I was on my own.

I lay in bed wondering what I was going to see tonight. Maybe nothing? Maybe Simon really was ill and was fast asleep now?

Maybe.

I heard my parents trudge up the stairs. And Muffin made a brief appearance. She didn't stay tonight though.

I parted the curtains a little bit. A grey mist looked in on me. I could hardly see anything or hear anything either – just the occasional yelp from one of the dogs next door.

My eyes began to feel heavy. I decided I'd just rest my eyes for a moment. I climbed back into bed and immediately fell asleep.

I felt guilty when I woke up; Jeff would be

very disappointed with me. I should get out of bed and watch again. But I was also very sleepy and my bed was warm and soft.

It was then I heard it.

A howling noise.

I tumbled out of bed and over to the window again. But I couldn't see a thing. The mist had swallowed everything up. Simon's garden had vanished. Even the howling had stopped as suddenly as it had begun. But I couldn't lose the feeling that something was out there crouching in the darkness.

And then out of the mist sailed what looked like a large white bubble. It cast an eerie paleness over everything. Now I could see . . . I could see there was someone in that garden.

CHAPTER SIX

I couldn't see the figure in the garden very clearly. But I knew it was Simon. He was standing very still underneath a tree in the middle of the garden.

My hand shaking, I reached for the binoculars. It was hard to hold them steady and the moon was already slipping away again.

Just for a moment I saw Simon's face, half-lit by the moonlight, half in darkness. But I saw enough.

I saw that hair had grown right across Simon's eyebrows and his chin. I saw there

95

was hair covering his ears and he had what looked like massive sideburns too. Only all the hair seemed to hang off Simon's face as if it didn't quite fit him.

My skin went cold. He looked hideous. He was a freak, a monster. There were no other words to describe him.

Then he tilted his head upwards towards my room. Had he seen me? I let go of the curtains. The binoculars jumped out of my hands. My legs wobbled. I fell on top of my bed.

Had he seen me? The question tore around my head. I felt he could still see me.

For ages I was too scared to move. I just sat there. My window was still open. But all I could hear was the blood pumping in my head.

Finally I got up and drew back the

curtains a centimetre. And then another centimetre. The moon was hidden once more. All I could see now was the mist pressing against the window.

It was almost as if I'd dreamt what I'd seen. But I knew I hadn't. And I knew I'd never forget what I saw, not if I lived to be a hundred and forty.

I felt sick – not with fear but with disappointment. Jeff was right: Simon really was a werewolf. Simon had lied to me. He'd probably only pretended to be my friend to keep me quiet.

Of course his family were in on it as well. I remember now how they had cross-examined me about my bedroom and whether I was a light sleeper. Maybe they were werewolves too: a whole nest of werewolves living next door to me. Goosebumps ran up my arms.

I pictured the three of them sitting round the table tonight . . . all heavily bearded. That was such a weird image I started to laugh softly.

Then I thought of Simon again, and his pretending to be my friend.

97

I got up and rustled through my special drawer. I brought out the wrapper from the box of chocolates he had given me. And I tore it up into tiny pieces. Then I got into bed again and wrote down everything I'd seen tonight in Jeff's log-book. In giant capitals at the end, I wrote:

NOW I KNOW FOR CERTAIN SIMON IS A WEREWOLF

CHAPTER SEVEN

In the dark the phone rang loudly and urgently. I squinted at my watch; it was exactly seven o'clock in the morning. No-one ever rings at that time unless it's something very serious.

But what? Maybe . . . maybe Simon's told his parents that I know he's a werewolf? So now they're ringing to tell my parents they'd better keep me quiet or else?

I crept to the top of the stairs. Normally when my dad answers the phone his voice booms around the house. But today I could hardly hear him. Then he put the phone down and started whispering to Mum.

'Who was that on the phone?' I called. I wanted to know – and yet in a way I didn't.

There was some more whispering and then Mum came upstairs. She sat on my bed with me. 'That was Nan's next-door-neighbour. Your nan had gone outside to feed the birds first thing in the morning as usual, when she had a fall.'

'Is she all right?'

'Yes,' replied Mum firmly. 'But your dad and I will be going down to see her and we might bring Nan back for a few days.'

I nodded gravely.

Usually I just have cereal for breakfast but today Dad made some hot buttered toast and the three of us sat around the kitchen table talking about Nan. Mum and Dad kept saying how strong Nan was, and telling funny stories about her.

'Don't you worry now, Kelly,' said Dad. And I suddenly realized they were both staring at me.

'You do look pale this morning,' said Mum.

'I always look pale,' I muttered. 'Ghosts envy me my complexion, you know.'

Mum ignored this. 'There's nothing else worrying you, is there, dear?' she persisted.

Only that I know for certain our next-door-neighbour is a werewolf, that's all. I longed to tell my parents the whole story. For the secret was now like a giant heavy weight dragging me down. But I knew this wasn't the right moment. I decided I would definitely tell my parents tonight: whether Nan was here or not.

Mum and Dad were outside packing the car when I heard Mum say, 'Oh, I'm sorry to hear Simon isn't very well.' I went outside to discover Mum talking to Mrs Doyle, with the two West Highlands bounding around their feet.

'Well, I do hope Simon's better soon,' went on Mum, giving me a 'I'm surprised you didn't tell me' look.

I quickly scrutinized Mrs Doyle's face for any sign of a beard. To my disappointment I couldn't see any.

'Hello, Kelly,' she said to me. But her smile wasn't as friendly as usual. 'I was just telling your mum about Simon not being well.'

'I heard,' I snapped. I wasn't going to pretend with her. We both knew the real reason why Simon wasn't going to school. Then feeling suddenly daring, I said, 'Could I see him for a moment please?'

Mrs Doyle's eyes wobbled. 'I'm sorry, Kelly, but he's asleep.'

'Are you sure?' I replied. Mum gave a little protesting cry at my rudeness. But I didn't care. Soon my mum would discover our neighbours' terrible secret.

'He's fast asleep,' replied Simon's mum firmly. 'But I'll tell him you called.'

'Yes, do that, won't you,' I replied, then walked off.

'Take care, Kelly,' Mrs Doyle called after me. I didn't like the way she'd said 'take care'. Was that another threat?

In the house Mum came up to me. 'Is everything all right between you and Simon?' she asked.

'No, Mum, it isn't,' I mumbled. 'But it's a long story, so I'll tell you about it tonight.'

Before Mum could reply Dad bounded in. Jeff had called. He was going back to school today. And Dad said he would give us both a lift.

In the car Jeff and I talked in a kind of code. 'How's Simon?' he asked.

'He's still not himself,' I replied. Then I said, 'Here's the notes you missed, Jeff,' and handed him the notebook. Jeff read avidly what I'd written down last night. He couldn't say anything. He just looked at me and mouthed, 'Wow!'

As we walked into school Jeff said, 'This is a really amazing discovery. You know, this could make us quite famous . . . if we live to tell the tale.'

There wasn't time to talk any more. School was freezing that day and lots of pupils were complaining. In the end we were allowed to keep our coats on during lessons. Then, just before lunch, there was an emergency assembly. The whole school jostled into the sports hall where, to loud cheers, the deputy headmistress announced that the heating had broken down and so everyone – apart from Year Eleven – had to go home. Then, to equally loud groans, she announced that school should be back to normal tomorrow. Still, a half-day's holiday was not to be sneezed at.

Jeff and I raced out of school and back to my house to work out a plan of action. 'The big problem,' said Jeff, 'is still getting anyone to believe us.'

We went up to my bedroom. I glanced idly out of my window, never suspecting . . . I spotted Simon out of the corner of my eye first. He was sitting cross-legged on the grass with all four dogs gambolling around him. The hair around his face looked even thicker that it had last night. And it was more shocking seeing him in the daylight somehow. It was like having a nightmare in the middle of the afternoon. I was about to alert Jeff. But there was no need.

'Look!' cried Jeff in a strange, hoarse voice. His eyes kept darting between me and what was outside the window. 'Look!' he repeated. Then he suddenly gripped my arm tightly and started pulling me away from the window. 'Got to be careful,' he stuttered. 'Werewolves have got hyper-hearing. Maybe he can hear us now.' Then he went and sped down the stairs and into the kitchen. I was right behind him.

Without a word Jeff filled up a glass of water. His hand shook as he gulped the water down. Then he turned to me. His eyes had gone all glassy. 'Never thought I'd see that . . . not in real life,' he whispered.

'Jeff, come and sit down.' He looked as if he was about to pass out.

Jeff fell on to a chair.

'And I'm sure he can't hear us otherwise he wouldn't be in his garden, would he?' I said.

Jeff looked up. 'That's true . . . he thinks we're still at school . . . and where do you reckon his parents are?'

'Well, I know his dad leaves for work very early and his mum helps out at the dog sanctuary part-time. She's always going on about it – and how important it is . . . what?'

For Jeff had suddenly stood up. 'I've just had a brilliant idea . . . why don't we take a picture of the werewolf?'

'What, from my bedroom window?'

'No, it's a bit far away. We could climb up the fence.'

'Climb?' I exclaimed.

'Or . . . or one of us could sit on the other's shoulders, quickly snap a picture and that's all the evidence we need. They'll have to believe us then.'

We gazed at each other excitedly. It sounded almost too easy.

'There's just one small problem,' I said. 'I haven't got a camera.'

'You must have.'

'I'm sorry, I haven't. My dad has one some-where but I'm pretty sure it hasn't got a film in it as . . .'

'We've got a camera,' interrupted Jeff, 'and it's a polaroid so you have your pictures right away. I'll go and get it?'

'Yeah, but be quick, won't you. He could go back inside at any minute.'

Jeff wiped his forehead. 'All right, don't keep on . . . all this stress. I still can't believe it. Him just sitting in the garden in his jeans and T-shirt. Him – a werewolf.'

'Jeff,' I cried urgently.

'OK, don't worry, I'll run my fastest.'

I tried to look impressed. But Jeff always came last in cross-country.

I watched him wobbling and wheezing down the road. Then I darted upstairs to check the werewolf was still in the garden. He was – but for how much longer?

Hurry up, Jeff.

Finally he came panting into view with a large camera round his neck. I opened the door and Jeff practically fell inside. His breath came in hurried gasps. He managed to say, 'Sorry I'm late . . . it was my mum . . . wanted to know why I wanted the camera.'

'What did you tell her?'

Jeff turned bright red. 'I told her I wanted to take a picture of you . . . it was all I could think of.'

'So when you go home with a picture of a werewolf . . .'

'She'll say, "Oh what a nice picture of Kelly. She's much more attractive than she used to be."' We grinned at each other for a moment. 'Is he still outside?' asked Jeff.

'He was the last time I looked.'

Jeff handed me the camera. 'There's only two pictures left by the way.'

'So I'm taking the picture, am I?'

Jeff shrugged. 'Well I thought it would be best as you're the lightest.' He paused.

'Yes, OK.' I took the camera. 'So what do I press, this button here?'

'Yeah, that's right. It's dead easy.' Then he added, 'When we're in your garden we mustn't talk. We must move like shadows.'

We didn't say a word until we reached the fence. 'Ready,' whispered Jeff. I swallowed hard, and nodded. He knelt down. I took my shoes off.

I climbed on to his shoulders. As he straightened up again, he hissed, 'You're much heavier than you look.'

'Sssh.'

'And did you know your feet smell?'

'They do not,' I hissed back indignantly. 'And stop shaking about.'

'Just hurry up, will you? I can't hold you for much longer.'

Now I could see over the fence. Simon was curled up on the grass. His eyes were closed. One of the West Highlands had snuggled down against his knees, while Plute was lying next to Simon's head.

'Come on,' whispered Jeff.

I aimed the camera. I wanted to get as much of Simon's face in as possible, and those werewolf hands too.

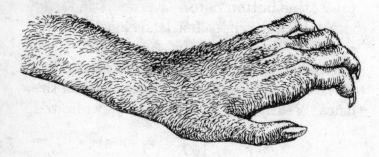

Plute's ears pricked up. He saw me. He gave a low growl. Simon muttered something to him. He sounded half-asleep. But I knew I had to take the picture now.

I pressed the switch just as Simon suddenly bolted upright. There was a great flash of light. Simon's eyes popped wide open as if I'd just shot him. He gave a great howl of pain. Then he fled into his house with the dogs barking beside him.

All at once I felt myself wobbling. Then I tumbled on to the grass.

'Sorry,' said Jeff apologetically. 'But I couldn't hold you a second longer . . . Still, you got it, didn't you?' Jeff pulled the photo out of the camera.

He waved it about in the air. 'This helps it develop . . . but I think we should look at it inside.'

Scrambling into my shoes, I followed Jeff into the kitchen where we peered at the picture. Nothing seemed to be happening to it.

'I've just thought . . . maybe you can't take pictures of werewolves because they're dead,' said Jeff.

'It's vampires who are dead, not were-wolves,' I replied snappily. 'Werewolves are . . . well, they're not dead anyway.' Then I cried, 'Look, something's happening.'

'Hey, I can see him,' said Jeff excitedly.

It was Simon's eyebrows which came out first, so bushy they seemed to have been joined together. Then those great clumps of hair which looked so weird hanging off an eleven-year-old's face.

'I wonder what it's like growing that enormous beard overnight. Hey, will you look at his eyes. He looks as if he's about to attack someone . . . probably you, and that camera.'

'I think he was just very shocked,' I said.

'And you've got one of his paws in too . . . that's not a bad picture at all, Kelly. I mean, you might have got a bit closer but actually we have all the evidence we need now. We've done it.'

We looked at each other.

'So now we can tell people,' went on Jeff.

'We are doing the right thing, telling people, I mean?' I asked.

'Kelly, he's a werewolf,' cried Jeff. 'What

about if he attacks someone? We'd feel really guilty then.'

I agreed with him, but I still had this horrible, sick feeling in the pit of my stomach.

'Shall I tell my mum then?' asked Jeff.

'Yeah, your mum will know what to do.' I closed my eyes for a moment. I felt dizzy. 'It's up to her now.'

'Are you sure you'll be all right here?'

'Oh yes.' I looked at my watch. 'Besides, my parents will be home soon.'

'And you will be careful about opening the door, won't you?' said Jeff anxiously.

I nodded. Then I asked, suddenly, 'What do you think will happen to Simon?'

'I don't know, maybe he'll be put in a zoo.'

'Locked up, you mean?'

'Well, you couldn't have tigers roaming the streets, could you? And he's much worse,' said Jeff. He got up. 'Remember, don't answer the door until you're certain who it is . . . If it's me I'll ring on the doorbell four times at once.' He gazed down at the photograph. 'Even now,' he said, 'I still can't believe it . . . a real-life werewolf living next door to you.'

After he'd gone I closed my eyes again. I felt strangely drowsy and drifted off to sleep. I dreamt I visited Simon at the zoo. It felt really bad until he escaped and started chasing me. The doorbell made me leap to my feet. It only rang once, so it couldn't be

Jeff. I stumbled to the door. 'Who is it?' I cried, as bravely as I could.

There was a pause, then, 'It's me, Simon. Let me in.'

'No, no. Go away.'

'Come on, Kelly, let me in . . . it's dangerous for me to be on your doorstep like this.'

'Dangerous for who?' My voice came out in a kind of croak. 'I've got nothing to say to you . . . just go.'

Then there was silence. Had he gone? I stood waiting, but I couldn't hear anything else. My knees were still shaking. I sat down, then almost at once I shot to my feet. What was that banging noise? It seemed to be coming from the garden. I rushed to the window in the dining room just as Simon leapt over the fence and into my back garden.

CHAPTER EIGHT

Simon was in my garden.

I felt scared and helpless. If he could leap over fences what else could he do?

I stared out of the window at him. He came closer. Then his face was right up against the glass.

I thought I was going to scream. But I didn't. I just stood there whimpering with fear, like some terrified puppy.

'Let me in, Kelly.'

It was so odd hearing Simon's voice coming out of a face which was not Simon's at all. It was as if he was wearing a terrible mask. And any second now he'd peel it off, and there would be Simon back again. But this wasn't any mask. He really was a . . .

'Get away, you werewolf, get away!' I cried.

At once he stepped back from the glass. Then he let out the loudest, most terrible howl I'd ever heard. It seemed to make the whole house shake. I started to shake too.

'Just go away!' I screamed. I sprang forward and started drawing the curtains. Then I rushed around the rest of the house frantically drawing the other curtains too.

There was silence. Had the werewolf

jumped back to its own garden? Or was it still hiding out there somewhere, just waiting for me to venture outside and then . . .?

He only needs to scratch you and you'd be a werewolf too. Wasn't that what Jeff had said? So I didn't dare go anywhere. I was trapped in this dark, shadowy house.

Oh, where was Jeff?

Why weren't he and his mum round here now? I ran to the phone and dialled Jeff's number. Let him be at home. Please let him be at home.

There was no reply.

Perhaps he and his mum were on their way round here?

But I had to talk to someone now. My mum and dad. How I wished I'd told them before. Nan's number was there by the phone. So I rang it.

There was no reply.

That must mean my parents were on their way home. But how much longer would they be? I didn't think I could stand another moment here alone.

Then the doorbell rang – three times.

Could that be Jeff? It'd be just like him to forget the code is four times not three.

It must be Jeff.

I raced to the front door. 'Who is it?'

No answer. Then the letter-box was pushed open. 'Kelly, open the door, please,' called a voice. It was Simon's mum. She scared me nearly as much as Simon.

'Just go away!' I screamed. 'My parents will be back any minute,' I added.

'We must talk first,' said Simon's mum, firmly. 'Come on, open the door at once.' Her tone was pleading yet I sensed she was angry with me too.

'No,' I began, then I stopped. I remembered something which made my blood turn to ice: Simon's mum had got a key. She and my mum exchanged keys, didn't they.

Then I heard a key turn in the lock.

CHAPTER NINE

The front door opened. I wanted to rush upstairs and hide in my bedroom. I nearly did. But then I thought, this is my house so why should I run away. Instead, I stood by the stairs gripping the bannisters tightly.

Simon's mum was standing in the hallway trying to smile reassuringly at me.

'Get out of my house now!' I cried.

'Yes, I will go, and I haven't closed the front door so you're perfectly safe,' she replied. 'But first you must let me explain . . .'

'Why?' I interrupted rudely. 'So you can tell me some more lies?'

'Kelly, whatever you think I just beg one thing of you – that picture you took, please don't show it to anyone. At least promise me that.' She sounded really scared. This made me feel a little braver.

'Answer me this first,' I said. 'Simon is a werewolf, isn't he?'

She took a sharp intake of breath, then whispered, 'Werewolf is such an ugly, melodramatic word. We never use it. But yes . . . my son is a wolf-boy.'

I began to feel afraid again. 'How long has he been one?'

'You're born a wolf-boy, Kelly. There's no other way. All those lurid stories in the cinema about people being bitten by wolves and turning into wolf-men is just nonsense

. . . dangerous nonsense. It causes such pain to us when, in fact, being a wolf-man is a calling, something to be proud of: the most wonderful gift. Simon's great-grandfather on my side was a wolf-man, so we hoped Simon might . . .'

'You hoped?' I said, disbelievingly. 'But look what happens to him . . .'

'Is his face so terrible?' she asked.

The question embarrassed me. I wasn't sure how to answer her.

'No-one's allowed to be different, are they?' went on Mrs Doyle.

'I didn't say that.'

'I think you did. You know, Kelly, when I was about thirteen I found my face was covered in spots. Those spots lasted for about two years and I felt so self-conscious about them. I'd see people turning away from me in the town. Even friends didn't seem to want to be my friends any more. Everyone changed, except me. I was the same person I'd been before . . . Simon's never had a spot in his life. But for about two or three years certain full moons cause hair to form all over his face and body — for a

couple of days. By tomorrow most of that hair will have disappeared. And by the time he's sixteen the hair on his hands will all have gone too. He may still have to shave two or three times a day, rather than once, when there's a full moon . . .'

'But otherwise he'll be normal,' I interrupted.

'Well, often wolf-men remain superior athletes – and it's not just during a full moon they can run faster, and jump higher than any man – and their hearing and sense of smell remains as sharp as any dog's. But they always use their superior powers to help mankind. Always,' she repeated, 'but then wolf-men are braver and more loyal than any mere man could be.'

The front door suddenly swung open.

Simon stood in the doorway.

'What are you doing out of the house

124

again?' exclaimed his mum. 'You, you know how dangerous it is for you.'

'I'm all right,' he said quietly. Then he looked across at me. 'Mum has told you the truth, hasn't she?'

I nodded.

'I'm glad,' he said. 'I wanted Mum to tell you.'

'It was Simon's idea I come round,' said his mum.

'I knew you wouldn't listen to me. I knew you were scared of me.' There was more than a hint of bitterness in Simon's voice. I couldn't look at him. I just kept staring at the carpet. I felt all twisted up inside.

'I warned Simon not to go in the garden on any account. But he so loves to be outside at this time and as you were all away he thought it was completely safe. I told him there's never a time during the day when it's completely safe, didn't I, Simon?'

'Yes, Mum,' said Simon absently. I knew he was staring at me. But I still couldn't look at him. Then Simon walked slowly towards me. When he was standing right in front of me he unclenched his right paw; I saw there a medal attached to a dark blue ribbon. 'I wanted to show you this . . . you can look at it if you like.'

I shivered slightly as my hand touched the hair on Simon's hand. But then I stared down at the medal. It was gold, although a bit tarnished. On one side was the profile of a king and on the other was what looked like an angel with arms outstretched. Around the edges of the medal was printed: AWARDED TO SIMON GARSON FOR BRAVERY OCTOBER 1919.

'My great-grandad,' said Simon. He spoke very quietly but there was no mistaking the pride in his voice.

'Simon's great-grandad helped track down some of the country's most dangerous criminals,' went on Simon's mum. 'Without him, many more people might have lost their lives.'

I kept on staring at the medal. To be honest, I didn't know what to say. 'Thanks for letting me see this,' I said finally. I handed the medal back to Simon. 'Do you want to be a detective like your great-grandad?' I asked.

'No, I want to help find people. At the moment I only have special powers – special animal powers – during a full moon. But later they'll be mine all the time. Then I'll just have to smell something and be able to track someone from hundreds of miles away. So I want to find people who go missing. I'd really love to do that.' He sounded so eager and enthusiastic, so like the Simon I'd first met that I suddenly looked up at him and into those dark, green eyes. And it was there I found Simon again. He'd been there all the time, of course. But it was only now I could see him again.

'I'm so sorry,' I cried.

'What for?'

'For not trusting you.'

'I don't blame you,' he began. 'It was only when you thought I'd killed that bird . . . you really upset me then . . . I wanted to tell you the truth from the start, you know.'

'But I wouldn't let him,' said Mrs Doyle. 'That was my one condition when we moved here. You see, Simon had never been to school before.'

'Never!' I exclaimed.

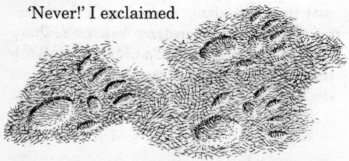

His mum smiled faintly. 'Simon has spent all his life at a special home for wolf-boys, far away from prying eyes. His father and I would visit him – and stay over at weekends. But Simon was so eager to go out into the world and go to a real school . . .'

'I read every school story there ever was,' he interrupted. 'I was just desperate.'

I said, 'That first day when you called for

me I thought you seemed a bit over-eager.'
We both grinned at the memory.

'When his father got a new job near here
we saw this house to let and, more to the
point, so did Simon. He begged and begged
us for his chance. We wanted to, of course,
but we also knew how very, very dangerous
it was.' She lowered her voice. 'If the world
found out about Simon's powers some
unscrupulous men could try and use him for
their own evil purposes . . .' She shook her
head. 'Sometimes men can be much more
dangerous than any dog – or wolf.' She
paused. 'And then there are other people
who would want to lock Simon away because
he was different . . . that is why, Kelly, I do
beg you not to show that photograph to
anyone.'

'But of course,' I began, then, with a jolt of
horror I remembered I didn't have the
picture: Jeff did. Goodness knows how many
people he'd have shown the photograph to by
now.

What could I do?

'Kelly, are you all right? You look a bit
groggy,' said Simon. His voice was gentle

and concerned. 'Do you want to sit down?'

'Yes, yes,' I said. Maybe I could think better sitting down. So many thoughts were whirling around in my head.

So I sat on the couch while Simon and his mum sat opposite me. Then Simon asked, 'Do you mind if I sit on the carpet? I find it more comfortable – at the moment.' He sat cross-legged on the carpet, then looked up at me. 'Go on then, ask me anything.'

'Anything at all?'

'Yes. I want to tell you everything now,' he cried.

I considered. There were so many things I wanted to ask him. 'That howling at night; it was you, wasn't it?'

He nodded. 'That huge kennel you saw, that's like my other bedroom. I'm always out there during a full moon. I do try to be considerate but howling at night, it's such a natural thing for me . . . like singing or whistling or playing the drums – only much, much better, especially during a full moon.'

'What does a full moon feel like then?'

'Well, even if it's the middle of winter you wake up thinking it's a boiling hot summer's

day, you just cannot get cool . . . that's the
first sign. Often that's the only one. But then
you have the odd full moon which really gets
you: then you start to burn up. That's what
happened to me at school yesterday. I've
never been as hairy as this before,' he added
apologetically. 'I've even got hair all down
my back this time. Still, it does have its brilliant side too. I mean, your sense of smell is
so strong you can smell everything, you can
even . . . you can even smell the seasons
changing. That's why I spend all night in the
kennel during a full moon. It's so intoxi-
cating out there, Kelly.'

'I can imagine,' I replied. And I could. I

was picturing it all. And I was so happy until a swift, dark cloud came over me blocking out everything . . . THE PHOTOGRAPH. I had to warn him. But the words didn't want to leave my throat.

'I'm sorry, we must stop there, we have to go,' said Mrs Doyle. 'It isn't safe for Simon to be out of the house today.'

'But can't I just stay a few more minutes?' said Simon. 'It gets so lonely shut away on my own.'

'No, Simon, I'm sorry,' replied Mrs Doyle firmly. Then she added more gently, 'Maybe Kelly could come and see us later. Maybe. Now I shall just check it's all clear outside . . . when I come back be ready to leave at once, Simon.'

'Mum,' Simon called after her. But she had already gone. He shrugged his shoulders. 'I just wanted to tell her – it's too late.'

'Too late?' I echoed.

'Listen,' he said.

Then I heard it – and saw it too. My parents' car pulling into the drive. 'Oh no, what are we going to do?' I cried.

'I don't know,' said Simon lightly. He didn't look scared at all.

'You must hide,' I said.

'Oh yes, I must hide,' he said slowly. 'But don't worry, I know all about hiding.

Outside a car door slammed shut. I saw my mum. Then I saw my nan struggling out of the car. I began to panic now. What would Nan do if she saw Simon – fall down in a dead faint?

'Simon, you'd better hide in my room,' I said.

'Sure, OK,' he said, but he didn't exactly rush up the stairs, and he gave me this sad grin as if to say, 'This is all so silly, isn't it?'

The doorbell rang. I sprang forward. Mum was helping Nan up the four steps to our door. 'As you can see, Kelly, your nan's come to stay for a few days.'

'Hello, Kelly,' said Nan, extending a hand

as tiny as a doll's to me. She was a dwarfish figure with wispy hair that was still a beautiful auburn colour and eyes as bright as a bird's. As usual, she was wearing a hat; this one had on it the longest feather I'd ever seen.

'All this fuss. I just slipped on the step, that's all,' muttered Nan. 'Could have happened to anyone.'

'Now you come and sit down,' said Mum, helping Nan over to the sofa. 'You've drawn the curtains a bit early, haven't you, Kelly? Draw them back, will you, dear.'

In a kind of daze I drifted to the window. Light poured into the room again. My mum was chattering on. 'Now I'd better go and pick your father up from the supermarket. He should have got everything by now. Then we'll unpack your bags, Nan. Now, will you be all right?'

'Of course I will,' replied Nan brusquely.

'Kelly will make you a nice cup of tea – and if you'd like to go up to your room Kelly will help you, won't you, dear?'

I nodded. My mum drove away. I smiled at Nan. 'Would you like a cup of tea?'

'No thank you.'

Then the phone rang. I hoped and hoped it was Jeff. It was Mrs Doyle.

'Kelly, you must get Simon out of the house.'

'Yes I know. I'll do my best,' I whispered.

'I'll be waiting outside,' she said.

'OK, I'll be as quick as I can. Bye.'

'What's going on? Who are you whispering to?' demanded Nan.

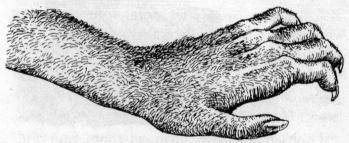

'Oh, just a friend,' I croaked. 'Are you sure you don't want a cup of tea?' Nan didn't answer. But she kept staring at me. Dare I try and get Simon out now?

And then from upstairs came the unmistakeable sound of a sneeze.

I stood there for a moment, horror-stricken. But Nan didn't appear to have heard anything. I started to breathe again.

Until Nan announced suddenly, 'I think I'd like to go upstairs. Will you help, Kelly?'

'Of course, Nan,' I said. Nan leant on me, although she wasn't heavy at all. We slowly walked up the stairs. My mind was racing. Once Nan was safely in her room, that would be the ideal moment for Simon to creep downstairs.

I helped Nan into the guest-room. She said she didn't want to sit down just yet. But she'd love a glass of water. I sped off to get her one, while Nan immediately started nosing around. For of course she'd heard that sneeze. And now she was doing some investigating of her own. She didn't have to look very far.

I rushed back upstairs. Then I nearly dropped the glass of water with shock. I could hear Nan's voice. And Simon's. Trembling, I opened my bedroom door. Nan immediately turned round and beamed at me. 'At last I've seen one. I've seen a wolf-boy,' she cried in a voice full of wonder, as if she'd just discovered a mermaid or a unicorn in my bedroom. She turned to Simon who was sitting on the carpet, grinning all over his face. 'I'm so glad I've been spared to see this day. When I was a little girl my parents would tell me stories about the wolf-men and all the crimes they solved and how we could all sleep safer in our beds because of them. I longed to see one but I never did. Sometimes, late at night I'd hear them though. And once I saw this light far away in the Cornish hills and my friends told me that's where the wolf-boys lived.'

'That's right,' said Simon. 'There's a special home for wolf-boys . . . that's where I lived, actually.'

'I wish I'd heard those stories about the wolf-men, Nan,' I said.

'Didn't your dad ever tell you them?' Nan shook her head. 'But then I should have told you them myself . . . It's such a shame when the old stories get lost,' she added, more to herself than us.

Feeling embarrassed and ashamed, I said, 'The thing is, Nan, I didn't know about wolf-men so I . . .' Then I started telling her what Jeff and I had done. When I mentioned the photograph Nan interrupted sharply, 'Where is it now?'

'It's safe with Kelly,' said Simon. Suddenly he was looking at me, his eyes shining out of the dark. And I thought, if I could wish for one thing in the world it would be for that picture. Then I'd hand it straight to Simon – or burn it, or do whatever he wanted. I wondered what Jeff had done with it. I must find him. Where was he?

Nan was already urging us towards the door. 'It seems so rude to push you away, wolf-boy, and there's so much I want to ask you. But it's best you spend tonight in your house away from prying eyes.'

'I know,' said Simon. 'But it's been really great to meet you.'

Nan gave a wizened chuckle. 'This has been such a wonderful surprise. I couldn't be more excited if Sherlock Holmes himself had walked in here.' She waved us off from the top of the stairs. 'I'll be all right here . . . be careful now, wolf-boy.' Nan said the word 'wolf-boy' so reverently it was as if she were saying 'Your Majesty'.

'I'll just go and see if your mum's outside,' I said to Simon. It was then the doorbell rang. Four times. 'It's Jeff,' I gasped. I was so relieved. Now I could get the picture back from him. 'You'd better hide in the sitting-room, Simon.'

'Just think, I'll have hidden in every room in your house soon,' he replied, with a weary smile.

'Get rid of them,' hissed Nan from the top of the stairs.

'It's all right, Nan. I know who it is,' I said. I opened the door to see Jeff, his mum and someone else who I dimly recognized as Jeff's nosy neighbour, Mr Prentice. He was carrying a net.

I stared at him in amazement.

'It's in there, isn't it?' he said. 'I know it is.'

'I don't know what you're talking about,' I began. But then my attention was caught by Simon's mum, hovering in the driveway. It was at that moment Mr Prentice suddenly shot past me.

'No, wait. You can't go in there,' I cried. But I was too late. He was in there. He was in the sitting-room. Then he leapt about a metre into the air and started snorting through his nose like a horse. 'Mr Prentice,' I cried. 'I can explain.'

'Walk out calmly,' he gasped. 'Don't want to alarm it. No need to run now.' Then he vanished faster than a magician's handkerchief.

Simon stared after him. He smiled into his beard. 'Well, he didn't stay long, did he? I hope it wasn't something I said.'

CHAPTER TEN

Simon and I started to laugh. We weren't really laughing at his joke. It's just when I'm nervous or scared I'll laugh at anything. And right then we were both very nervous and very scared.

I saw the net which Mr Prentice had dropped on to the carpet in terror. 'And he says he used to stalk big game,' I said. 'I don't think so.' Simon and I laughed again, until suddenly I realized that net was meant for Simon. Simon could be sprawling around inside there now.

143

Simon looked at that net and shuddered. While in the hallway there were raised voices, Mrs Doyle saying, 'If you'll just calm down and let me explain.'

'No, I'm sorry, I can't calm down,' replied Jeff's mum. 'I just want to know exactly what's going on.' She marched into the sitting-room, saw Simon, and gave a horrified gasp. 'Is this some kind of prank you're all playing on my son? If so, I think it's in pretty poor taste. You've scared poor Jeff half to death.'

Jeff blushed deep red.

'Well, maybe your parents can explain what's going on,' went on Jeff's mum as a familiar car turned into our drive.

'They can't, but I can,' called a voice from the top of the stairs. 'Come on, help me down, Kelly.'

I helped Nan downstairs, just as my parents trooped inside. Dad was carrying a large box of shopping. He looked around in astonishment. 'We seem to have a full house.' He peered into the sitting-room, saw Simon and declared, 'Bit late for Halloween, isn't it?' Then he gave this apology of a laugh and froze. So did my mum.

Their faces seemed to be stuck in that horrified state until Nan said, 'I don't know why you're looking like that, son. I told you all about wolf-boys when you were little. Don't you remember?'

'Yes, I do,' said Dad. 'But I thought they were just stories.'

'Just stories,' said Nan in the same tone teachers use when you say the dog ate your homework.

'Well, no-one has ever told *me* any stories about wolf-boys,' said Jeff's mum. 'And I'm still waiting for an explanation.'

'I'll tell you all you need to know,' said Mrs Doyle. 'But only after you've put away that thing.' She nodded at the net. Dad hastily picked up the net and threw it in the back garden.

Then there was this great babble of voices as Nan and Mrs Doyle tried to explain while my parents and Jeff's mum kept inter-rupting. They seemed to be asking the same questions, over and over. Mrs Doyle was remarkably patient, I thought, but I noticed how her eyes kept darting out of the window. All the time she was watching, on the alert for danger.

Simon never said a word. He stood in the darkest corner of the room staring down at the carpet, as if he didn't want to hear what everyone was saying.

'Hello,' I whispered to him. 'How are you?'

'Dog-tired,' he replied, with a quick smile. 'I wish this was all over.'

I felt really sorry for him. I had to help him. But what could I do? There was one thing: give Simon the picture back.

I edged across to Jeff. 'They're giving me a headache,' moaned Jeff, nodding at his mum and my parents. 'Why are they asking so many questions? Are they going to write a fact-sheet on wolf-men or something? I understand it now. Why can't they?'

I nodded sympathetically, then asked,

'Can I have our photo back?'

He shook his head, regretfully. 'I'm afraid old man Prentice has got it.'

'Oh no. How could you give the photograph to Prentice?' I cried this out so loudly everyone turned around.

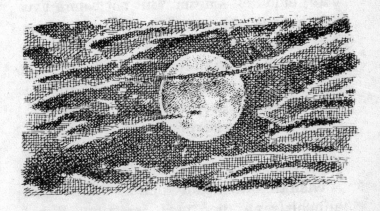

'What's this about the photograph?' demanded Mrs Doyle. 'I thought you had it, Kelly.'

'No,' I said miserably. 'I gave it to Jeff and he . . .'

'I gave it to Mr Prentice to look at,' interrupted Jeff's mum, 'as he knows about wild creatures and things . . . he examined the photograph through his magnifying glass for us to see if it was a fake. I mean, it could have been.'

'But we've got to get it back!' I exclaimed.

'Yes we have,' cried Mrs Doyle.

'I'm sure I shall be able to get the picture back from Mr Prentice without any problem at all,' said Jeff's mum. 'But not before I've had the answers to a few more questions from Mrs Doyle. There is the school, for instance. Now did they know . . .?'

'But there's no time for any of this,' I yelled. 'Really, there isn't.'

'Kelly, don't be so rude,' snapped my mum. She turned to Jeff's mum. 'I'm sorry, please finish what you were saying.'

'Thank you,' said Jeff's mum. She launched into her next question. But I noticed Simon was suddenly gazing all around him. He looked anxious. Then I saw why.

A large van was pulling up outside our house. Out of the van jumped two men in grey uniforms. They helped out of the van a third person: Mr Prentice. My heart started to thump. As all three walked quickly up our drive, I heard Mr Prentice saying, 'No, it lives next door but it was here earlier . . . of course, they may have evacuated the house.' Inside the sitting-room everyone had been startled into silence.

'If only you'd stayed inside, Simon, as you were told,' burst out Mrs Doyle, 'then none of this would have happened.'

'It's our fault, Kelly's and mine, not his,' said Jeff sadly. 'And yours,' he added, glaring at the adults, 'for just talking and talking all the time.'

The doorbell rang. 'I'll deal with this,' said Mrs Doyle, her voice strong again. My parents and Jeff's mum followed her to the door.

'You children stay here,' said Jeff's mum. She closed the sitting-room door but we could still hear . . .

'We're from the local authority, here is our I.D. We're concerned with exotic and dangerous creatures, and we're investigating a complaint that you are keeping a wild beast – without a licence – that is a threat to public safety. This is the picture we were given of it.'

'He must have the polaroid now,' hissed Jeff.

Then we heard Mrs Doyle say, 'That creature, I'm proud to say, is my son.'

'Good for you,' whispered Nan.

But the man went on, 'Do you have a licence for it, er, him?'

'Of course not,' said Mrs Doyle.

'And is he in the house now?'

'That's my business,' replied Mrs Doyle.

'We do need to see him,' the man persisted.

'It's the law,' said the other man.

'I've seen it, great terrifying thing it was,'

declared Mr Prentice, his voice carrying right down the road. 'And none of you are safe while this thing is roaming about.'

'Oh no,' I groaned. At the same moment Simon let out a low howl.

'Do you hear it?' shrieked Mr Prentice. 'Now do you believe me. I only escaped from it by the skin of my teeth. We're all in terrible danger.'

'Why won't he stop going on about it?' I hissed. 'He's getting everyone all wound up and . . .' I froze. I can't tell you how scary it is to look casually out of your window and see a face staring back at you. It was a man's face. He had cupped his hands and was peering intently at us.

'I think I can see something,' he called.

'Go away!' I screamed. 'Go away!'

'Or you're going to be really sorry,' added Jeff, after the man had gone.

'I don't believe that,' I exclaimed. 'The nerve of him, just barging up to our window like that.' The three of us looked at each other, shaken and incredulous.

'Now I know how animals in the zoo feel,' said Jeff, trying to make a joke of it. He and

I laughed uncertainly. 'We'd better draw the curtains over,' went on Jeff, 'just in case we get any more peeping toms.'

'No, it's all right, don't worry,' said Simon through clenched teeth. 'I've had enough. I'm going to sort this out.' Without another word he bolted past us.

'Simon, don't go out there,' I cried. Jeff and I rushed after him. But we were too late. Simon was already outside.

A large crowd was gathering. I recognized Rat-bag Sarah and her dad. There were cries of alarm when Simon appeared on the steps. Someone screamed and Sarah's dad jumped in front of her. Meanwhile the two men from the local authority looked as if they'd been hypnotized; they just stood there with their mouths open.

'Oh, Simon, why didn't you stay in the house?' cried Mrs Doyle.

'I'm just so tired of hiding, Mum,' replied Simon quietly. The crowd were backing further and further away. Most of them were huddling together in the middle of the road now. And they were eerily quiet, not saying a word. But their eyes were on stalks. They gawped and gawped at Simon until someone started to laugh. It was Sarah's dad. His laughter was loud and mocking.

'All right,' he said, 'it was a good joke. You had us all fooled, even me for a moment there. But you can take the mask off now.' That last sentence was more like a command.

Simon shook his head.

Sarah's dad came striding towards him. There were cries of alarm. But Sarah's dad just called out, 'We're all being played for fools. I'll show you what's going on. I'll bring that mask back with me.'

He was a large, paunchy man and he

153

towered over Simon. He wagged his finger reprovingly. 'You've had your fun but now I'm telling you again, lad, to take the mask off.' His voice was soft and confident.

Simon looked up at him with steady, green eyes. 'I promise you, it's not a mask,' he said.

'Of course it isn't,' added Mrs Doyle.

Sarah's dad leant forward as if he was going to whisper something in Simon's ear. Instead, he started pulling at Simon's beard. Immediately Mrs Doyle and me were yelling at him to stop. But Simon just stood there, not moving a muscle.

'What is going on here?' shouted Sarah's dad, tugging furiously at Simon's beard.

'You're hurting him,' I cried. 'Leave him alone.'

Sarah's dad finally stopped and staggered backwards. 'What is this?' he demanded angrily. 'We've a right to know.' But his voice had lost its pleased as punch smugness. And he was hissing fiercely, like a kettle about to boil.

'Answer him then,' called a voice from the crowd.

'Come on, speak,' cried someone else.

A ripple of wind ran through Simon's beard. And his head was tilted upwards slightly as if he were sniffing the air. I thought he looked magnificent. Then he raised his paw, at which there were more gasps. 'Please listen,' he said to the crowd. 'I may look strange to you – at first. But I come in peace.' He sounded as if he were a creature from another planet. Still, by the way everyone was staring at him, that was probably how he felt.

'I come in peace,' he repeated. 'And I can help you. I want to help you.'

'But you're a werewolf,' called a voice.

'Bolt all your doors tonight,' yelled Mr Prentice.

I shot him a look of utter contempt. But there were murmurs of agreement. 'Someone like you should be locked up,' said

155

a man, backing further away as he said it. There were even louder murmurs of agreement.

'No, look, please listen to me,' went on Simon. But his voice had sunk to a whisper. And then he just turned away. I don't think he could bear looking at that crowd any more.

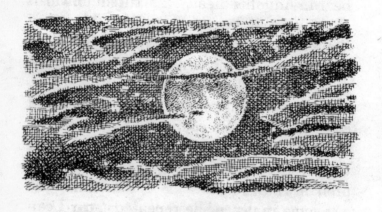

I thought, Simon has risked everything tonight. He could have just hidden in my house. But instead, he'd gone out there facing everyone, because he wanted them to understand. If only they'd give him a chance.

They must give him a chance.

I burst out, 'You say he should be locked

up. But why? Because he looks different to you and me. Some of us know Simon, and like him a lot.' I looked straight at Sarah. 'Now tonight he's got some hair on his face and his hands, but look closer, it's still Simon, our friend. So please listen to him. He really can help us and . . .'

'The fact is,' interrupted Sarah's dad – something of his oily, confident himself again, 'I cannot allow someone like this, someone who's only half-human, to go to school with my daughter. Anything could happen.'

Sarah stared up at him. 'Dad, shut up, will you,' she hissed.

I shot Sarah a grateful look, but her dad wouldn't be silenced. He carried on yelling as if a gale were raging round him. 'I'm sorry, we really can't allow a creature like this – however reasonable he might pretend to be – to roam around freely, can we?' Everyone in the crowd – apart from Sarah – seemed to agree with him.

Then one of the men from the local authority whispered to Mrs Doyle, 'I think it's best if we talk inside your house. We do need to ask a few questions.' He sounded quite apologetic about it.

'Yes, all right,' said Mrs Doyle. 'Come on, Simon, let's get this over with.'

'We'll come with you,' said my mum. 'You go and keep Nan company, Kelly.'

I turned to Simon, who still had his head averted from the crowd. 'Simon, I'm so sorry. I really never meant this to happen. You must believe that.'

Simon gave me this big, warm smile. 'See you soon,' he said. He sounded really bright and confident. But as he walked next door his shoulders sagged dejectedly and he kept his head right down, not looking at anyone.

I glared at the crowd. There were now about forty people thronging around. Sarah's dad was ranting on to anyone who would listen about 'our public duty', while a grim-faced Sarah stood beside him. I could even feel a tiny bit sorry for her.

Then I saw the other man from the local authority – the one who'd done most of the talking – dart into the van. I went over. Inside the van I saw a large cage. Was that cage meant for Simon? I looked at the man in alarm. As if reading my thoughts he jumped down and closed the van door. I think that was his little gesture to show he knew Simon wasn't dangerous.

I asked him, 'Have you still got the photograph?'

'Yes.'

'Could I have it, please . . . it is mine, you know.'

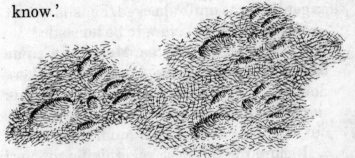

He hesitated, then handed it to me. 'Be very careful what you do with it, won't you?' he said.

'Oh I will,' I replied.

I was running into my drive when a bald-headed man from the crowd called out, 'Let's have a look at your picture, girlie.'

I shook my head and thrust the photograph down my pocket.

159

'You can make some money with that picture,' he went on.

'Leave her alone,' demanded an oddly commanding voice from the doorway. It was Nan.

I sped over to her. 'Did you see what happened, Nan?'

'I saw,' she replied bitterly, then she said, 'Let's go inside, shall we, love.' She said this so gently I was quite shocked. For she wasn't usually a very cosy Nan, to be honest.

I made Nan a pot of tea. My parents came back. 'There's someone from the zoo there now,' said Dad, 'and the police . . . I think they're going to be a while sorting all this out . . .' Then Jeff and his mum called in.

'I acted for the best,' said Jeff's mum. 'I really did.' She talked on and on again until finally Jeff stood up and announced, 'I want to apologize to Simon properly. Will you come with me, Kelly? We can tell him we've got the picture.'

'Sure, of course.'

But my dad said grimly, 'I don't think you'll get through. It's pandemonium out there.'

Dad was right. Now there were hordes of people jostling outside Simon's house. Where had they all come from? It was just like when there's a fight at school and hundreds of people suddenly appear out of nowhere. Only this crowd weren't yelling 'fight, fight, fight'; they were getting worked up about 'the unspeakable monster inside'. Several were waving cameras, while another was peering at the house through binoculars. How disgusting, I thought, until I remembered two nights ago I'd done exactly the same.

There was also a woman interviewing people in the crowd. I heard her call

out, 'Now, did anyone actually see this werewolf?'

Jeff and I pushed our way through. A policeman was now standing outside the door.

'Please let us in,' I said. 'We've got to see Simon.'

'Ah, everyone wants to see him.'

'But we're friends of his,' I cried.

'We need to tell him something important,' added Jeff.

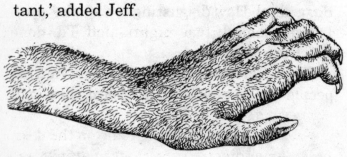

'I'm sorry,' said the policeman. 'But I've had strict instructions not to let anyone through at the moment.' Then he added, confidingly: 'There's a doctor in there; someone from the RSPCA; the local MP; while the boy's dad has just arrived . . . It's a real circus. Best talk to your friend tomorrow morning.'

We slowly walked back to my house. 'That's her,' cried a voice. 'She's the girl with a picture of the werewolf.'

The woman who'd been interviewing people sprang forward. She had a small, twitchy face and looked just like a hamster. 'Are you the girl who took the photo?'

'I might be.'

'Well, you've got a very valuable picture there. How about if I talk to you and your parents about it?'

'It's not for sale, is it?' said Jeff.

'That's right,' I replied.

We started to walk away.

'You're making a big mistake,' called the woman after us.

Seconds later she was ringing on the doorbell, demanding to talk to my parents and saying how I could name my own price. Mum soon got rid of her.

But Jeff said to me, 'I'm worried about that photograph . . . what if someone tries to steal it in the night? Who knows what people could do with it . . .? Then there would be pictures all over the place and you might have people turning up here wanting

163

to do experiments on Simon.'

The photograph proved surprisingly difficult to tear up. In the end Jeff and I took it in turns to cut the photo up into the tiniest of pieces. At last I felt we were doing something to help Simon – and put things right.

'Tomorrow, most of the hair from Simon's face will have gone,' I said. 'In fact, it's probably disappearing now.'

'So Simon can go back to school just as before, can't he?' said Jeff eagerly.

'There'll be some fuss at first,' I replied. 'And some people might act a bit funny and treat Simon as some kind of outcast.'

'Well, I know what that's like,' said Jeff, 'so I can give him a few tips. I tell you what, I'll come round early tomorrow and we can make plans: the three of us.'

We shook hands and made a pact, that we would never let Simon down again.

CHAPTER ELEVEN

Next morning I was woken up by someone tapping on my bedroom door. Before I could reply the door opened.

'Are you awake, Kelly?' called a voice I recognized instantly.

'Yes, Nan . . . what time is it?'

'It's quite late,' snapped Nan. But my nan's 'quite late' equals 'very early' for most people. Nan always says if she stays in bed past six o'clock it gives her a headache. I was still feeling drowsy when Nan said, 'I've heard them next door. They're up and about and I think they'd appreciate a visit.'

I was out of bed at once then. For I was desperate to talk to Simon. Jeff and I had tried ringing him several times last night but the phone had been continually engaged.

I hurriedly had a shower and got dressed.

Then I helped Nan down the stairs. 'How's your ankle this morning, Nan?' I asked, politely.

'More important things to think about than that,' said Nan. She hated it if you asked her questions about her health. 'Do you want anything to eat?' she asked.

'No thanks, I'm not hungry . . . I just want to see Simon.'

Nan nodded in approval. 'I expect we'll be

166

offered a cup of tea next door anyway.'

Just as Nan was putting her hat on, Dad's sleepy voice called downstairs, 'Is everything all right?'

'What do you think?' snapped my nan, and closed the door before Dad could ask any more questions.

Outside there was a smaller crowd than last night. But there were still about fifteen people hanging about. A couple were passing flasks around. Another was setting up a video camera.

When they saw Nan and me come out of our house there was a buzz of interest. People looked at us expectantly as if we were actors on a stage. Then Nan raised her hand and cried, 'Out of my way, shoo, shoo,' as if they were chickens. I nearly burst out laughing.

The policeman had gone now. So Nan rang on the doorbell. Immediately all the dogs started barking. They sounded particularly angry and upset today. Then the door opened a crack. Mrs Doyle saw who it was and opened the door a little wider.

'Come in, come in,' she said, and as quickly

as Nan could manage we squeezed inside. Then the door was firmly closed again. The four dogs wagged their tails cautiously.

'We just came round to see how you are,' said Nan.

'How are we . . . yes, how are we?' Mrs Doyle appeared on the verge of tears. But then she recovered herself. 'We're all right, really . . . come and have a cup of tea in the kitchen.'

'That would be very nice,' said Nan.

There was no sign of Simon, but Mr Doyle was sitting on the stairs talking into his mobile phone. He nodded at us as we went past. He was talking very quickly so I couldn't catch what he was saying.

But then in the kitchen I saw two cases. I let out a cry, then looked up at Mrs Doyle.

'Yes,' she said, gently. 'We're leaving.'

'But why?' I began, then realizing that was a silly question, I went on, 'I mean, I know why, but we can fight this. Jeff and I will go to school with Simon today . . . and we'll talk them round. You'll see.'

'I'm not sure how many other pupils will be there,' said Mrs Doyle dryly. 'The head-

168

master rang me last night; he was very nice about it, but he's had calls all evening from parents saying they will remove their children from school while someone who is a dangerous werewolf – as they persist in calling Simon – is attending.'

'But once they know the truth . . .' I exclaimed.

'At the moment they're just not listening,' said Nan, settling herself at the kitchen table.

'But they've got to listen,' I cried.

'And they will. In time,' said Mrs Doyle. 'We had someone from the government round here last night. They've known about wolf-men and all the wonderful things they've done for years. I told them it's time everyone knew the truth. He said he agreed with me, so some good might come out of this.'

'Where's Simon?' I asked suddenly.

'He's upstairs, packing,' replied Mrs Doyle. 'He's quite upset about all this,' she added quietly.

'Could I see him?' I asked.

'Best to leave him now,' replied his mum, gently. 'But I know he'll be coming round to see you to say goodbye.'

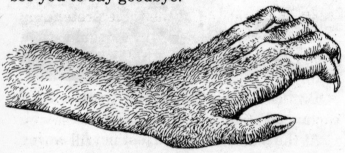

Goodbye. The word hammered away in my head blocking out everything else.

Later Nan and I walked back to my house. Nan seemed to be walking much more slowly now, her face almost touching mine. Tears started escaping down my face. 'Now what are you crying for?' said Nan indignantly. 'You've known a wolf-boy. There are very few human beings who can say that. You've been very lucky.'

'But Nan, he's leaving.'

'I know. But he has to go,' said Nan. 'For he wouldn't have much of a life here at the moment, would he? But he'll find you again. I am absolutely certain of that.'

Waiting in the doorway was Jeff. 'I couldn't sleep. How's Simon?' I didn't need to reply.

Jeff and I sat round the table pretending to eat breakfast. Neither of us could eat a thing. But we talked and talked . . . about Simon.

And then I had a terrible thought: what if Simon wanted to leave without saying goodbye to me? What if he was still angry with me? Was that why he hadn't come downstairs when I called?

I rushed to the front door. No; their car was still there. I watched Mr Doyle put some cases in the boot.

Then Mrs Doyle appeared with a bag. And finally, to my great relief, I spotted Simon.

There was a puzzled murmur of interest from the crowd as Simon jauntily strolled through them in his T-shirt and jeans. 'That can't be him,' called a voice. For practically all the hair had disappeared from his face. Now he just had a few bits of stubble on his chin, while his hands were hidden again in black gloves.

'Are you the werewolf?' shouted someone after him. Simon didn't appear to hear. And then I saw why; he had his headphones on. With something of a flourish he took the headphones off. 'Just came round to say cheerio for now,' he announced to Jeff and me.

'Are you the werewolf?' shouted someone again. This time Simon heard him. There was an awkward silence for a moment. Then

Simon grinned. 'Got them really confused, haven't I?'

Inside I said, 'I quite miss all your hair now.'

'Did it all just go at once?' asked Jeff.

Simon didn't seem at all embarrassed by the question. 'Pretty much . . . you get this tickling sensation on your face and down your back . . . goes on for about an hour. But it's a laugh too. Like shaving without having to switch on the razor.' He grinned at us again. 'Anyway, I'm afraid I've got to go in a minute.'

Jeff went over to Simon. 'I'd like to shake you by the hand,' he said.

Simon immediately extended a gloved hand. Jeff shook his head. Understanding, Simon took off one of his gloves. The thick, black hair and pointed fingernails were still there. And seeing them so suddenly again made me catch my breath. Just for second. But Jeff didn't show any hesitation at all. He clasped Simon's hand firmly. 'Look after yourself then,' he said.

'And you,' replied Simon.

Then Simon said goodbye to my mum and

dad and Nan – who gave him her address if he should ever be passing – after which they all left to see off Simon's parents.

Now Simon and I were on our own.

'I wish you weren't going,' I cried.

'I'll be back before you know it,' said Simon lightly. 'Soon people will know the truth about wolf-boys and how incredibly cute and lovable we are.'

'Modest too.'

He laughed, then dug into his pocket and produced a little box. 'And this is for you.'

I stared at the box for a moment.

'Open it then,' said Simon.

Inside was the medal belonging to Simon's great-grandad. I read again the words: AWARDED TO SIMON GARSON FOR BRAVERY OCTOBER 1919.

'But I can't take this,' I gasped.

'I reckon if my great-grandad had heard what you said to that crowd last night, the way you . . . well I know he'd want you to have it. And so do I.'

'Oh, Simon, it's the most wonderful present I've ever had.'

'Is it really?' He looked pleased. 'Anyway

I'd better go. Don't forget me, will you?'

Outside a man in a yellow anorak stopped Simon. 'You live next door to it?' said the man. 'So you must know what animal is in there.' He nodded at Simon's house.

'All right, I'll tell you,' said Simon. 'It's a giraffe.'

'Not really,' exclaimed the man, excitedly.

Simon turned round and winked at me.

Five minutes later Simon was sitting in the back of his car with the four dogs scrambling over him.

The car drove quickly away.

I ran after it, waving frantically. Simon opened the window. 'Look out for giraffes – and a wolf-boy,' he called.

And then the car vanished around a corner.

He was gone.

I could feel tears pricking at the back of my eyes. I felt so sad and alone until I remembered . . . *Look out for a wolf-boy*. That's what Simon had called out to me. He would find me again, wouldn't he, just like Nan said.

'Hurry back, Simon,' I whispered. And then I let out this great long howl. Simon was far, far away by now. But somehow I knew he'd heard me.

THE END

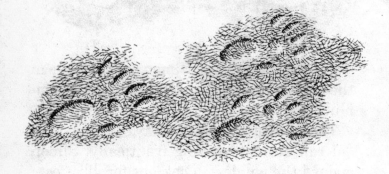